THE PROBLEMS OF DR. A

Also by Elizabeth Seifert

YOUNG DOCTOR GALAHAD
(Winner of $10,000 Prize)
A GREAT DAY
THUS DOCTOR MALLORY
HILLBILLY DOCTOR
BRIGHT SCALPEL
ARMY DOCTOR
SURGEON IN CHARGE
A CERTAIN DOCTOR FRENCH
BRIGHT BANNERS
GIRL INTERN
DOCTOR ELLISON'S DECISION
DOCTOR WOODWARD'S AMBITION
ORCHARD HILL
OLD DOC
DUSTY SPRING
SO YOUNG, SO FAR
TAKE THREE DOCTORS
THE GLASS AND THE TRUMPET
THE STRANGE LOYALTY OF DR. CARLISLE
HOSPITAL ZONE
THE BRIGHT COIN
HOMECOMING
THE STORY OF ANDREA FIELDS
MISS DOCTOR
DOCTOR OF MERCY
THE DOCTOR TAKES A WIFE
THE DOCTOR DISAGREES
LUCINDA MARRIES THE DOCTOR
DOCTOR AT THE CROSSROADS
MARRIAGE FOR THREE
A DOCTOR IN THE FAMILY
CHALLENGE FOR DR. MAYS
A DOCTOR FOR BLUE JAY COVE
A CALL FOR DR. BARTON
SUBSTITUTE DOCTOR
THE DOCTOR'S HUSBAND
THE NEW DOCTOR
LOVE CALLS THE DOCTOR

HOME-TOWN DOCTOR
DOCTOR ON TRIAL
WHEN DOCTORS MARRY
THE DOCTOR'S BRIDE
THE DOCTOR MAKES A CHOICE
DR. JEREMY'S WIFE
THE HONOR OF DR. SHELTON
THE DOCTOR'S STRANGE SECRET
LEGACY FOR A DOCTOR
DR. SCOTT, SURGEON ON CALL
KATIE'S YOUNG DOCTOR
A DOCTOR COMES TO BAYARD
DOCTOR SAMARITAN
ORDEAL OF THREE DOCTORS
HEGERTY, M.D.
PAY THE DOCTOR
THE RIVAL DOCTORS
DOCTOR WITH A MISSION
TO WED A DOCTOR
THE DOCTOR'S CONFESSION
BACHELOR DOCTOR
FOR LOVE OF A DOCTOR
A DOCTOR'S TWO LIVES
DOCTOR'S KINGDOM
DOCTOR IN JUDGMENT
THE DOCTOR'S SECOND LOVE
DOCTOR'S DESTINY
THE DOCTOR'S REPUTATION
THE TWO FACES OF DR. COLLIER
THE DOCTOR'S PRIVATE LIFE
THE DOCTOR'S DAUGHTER
DOCTOR IN LOVE
FOUR DOCTORS, FOUR WIVES
THE DOCTOR'S AFFAIR
THE DOCTOR'S DESPERATE HOUR
TWO DOCTORS AND A GIRL
THE DOCTORS ON EDEN PLACE
DR. TUCK
REBEL DOCTOR

THE DOCTORS WERE BROTHERS

THE PROBLEMS OF DR. A

Elizabeth Seifert

Dodd, Mead & Company
New York

Copyright © 1979 by Elizabeth Seifert
All rights reserved
No part of this book may be reproduced in any form
without permission in writing from the publisher
Printed in the United States of America

1   2   3   4   5   6   7   8   9   10

Library of Congress Cataloging in Publication Data

Seifert, Elizabeth, date
  The problems of Doctor A.

  I. Title.
PZ3.S4603Pr [PS3537.E352]   813'.5'2   79-11017
ISBN 0-396-07686-6

THE PROBLEMS OF DR. A

1

It was raining. And at four o'clock of an afternoon in early fall a fire glowed, comfortingly, on the hearth. And down the hill the lights of town bloomed rosily. The hospital was alight, of course, but Dr. Alster was off duty and he did not so much as glance at the big white stucco building, its deep porches dark and deserted on such a foul day.

There were a few people about. Some of the patients had grounds privileges, a few were allowed to go into town. And if one of these thought that he had an errand downtown, he would exercise his privilege and go down that steep hill to the dime store for his roll of cellophane tape, which he could have purchased in the hospital PX. The town's storekeepers knew the limits there were to the patients' shopping. After all, they were in this hospital because of mental disturbances, varying in intensity. They had no violents at Leland Haloran Hospital. Though, of course, sometimes . . .

"If it gets a little colder," said Dr. Alster, "there will be a great rattling of tire chains."

Jane nodded, her mouth full of something she was holding tight. Her husband had no idea what she was doing on that card table full of wire and weeds and chestnuts and acorns. And they both knew that the town was correct in demanding tire chains on the old, steep, narrow streets if there was ice or snow.

"Do you have rounds?" his wife asked when her mouth was free.

"Yes, but it's only four o'clock. And I may not go over at all."

He might not. Dr. Alster did pretty well what he pleased. He was the medical officer, not one of the neuropsychiatrists that, largely, staffed the hospital. Now he picked up the book that he had been reading and became absorbed in it. Jane thought it looked dreadfully dull. But Alster was different. She gazed at him intently. Was he *ever* different! The fact that she, and almost everyone else, called him Alster. Not Dick, or Richard, which was his proper name. Richard William Alster. Often, on the wards, he was called "Dr. A."

He signed everything, prescriptions, bank checks, even church registers, with the one word, Alster. And for him that seemed natural. Maybe he belonged here at this mental hospital. If being different had any significance.

Certainly he was an exciting man—Jane had discovered that quality on her first meeting with him, almost twenty years ago, and she had set out forthwith to know him better, to have him for a lover, and possibly a husband. Now she studied his well-known profile. Alster didn't change much. His hair was just as black; the last couple of years he had been wearing short sideburns; there was not a wrinkle in his lean, ascetic face; his jawline was firm, and his eyes as piercing as ever under his jutting brow and heavy black eyebrows.

"I don't think he's handsome," she thought, "but a woman picks him out in a crowd. Any crowd. He—"

"The Hulversons are coming," she said softly and rose to open the front door for the neighbors she had seen passing the wide window.

Alster sighed and set the thick book aside, rose to greet their guests.

"We smelled your fire," said Dr. Hulverson, coming in, "and it seems to be just the day for it." He hung his raincoat over the back of a chair, took his wife's poncho and draped it over a second one. The staff houses were all alike. A large room—mixed hall, living room, and dining room—a kitchen. Upstairs, two bedrooms and a bath.

They were pleasant houses, built as duplexes, with fenced patios at the rear. Some of the staff used the government-issue furniture, which was not bad, but the Alsters used their own, and on that dreary afternoon their living room glowed with color. A handsome Navajo rug covered one wall, there were paintings, full bookshelves—Jane in a blue jumpsuit that matched her eyes—and Alster's infallible hospitality and good manners.

"I would have loaned you a log and a match," he told Dr. Hulverson, giving him a glass.

"But would you have cleaned out the ashes tomorrow?" asked Carolyn. "He is always too busy to do that."

"Alster doesn't do it, either," said Jane. "He doesn't bother to find an excuse."

They settled companionably into the deep chairs and the big couch. Outside the window a cedar tree lashed in a rising wind, and rain rattled against the pane. Carolyn asked if Margaret would be coming home for Thanksgiving.

"—or for one of the breaks the schools always seem to be having."

"How do they have time to learn anything?" asked her husband.

"Oh, one pays tuition to get these modern kids out of

their parents' hair," said Alster in a reasonable tone. "One doesn't expect them to learn anything."

"Now, Alster," murmured Jane.

"Tell me what they learn!" the doctor persisted. "Take Margaret for an example. The dear Lord knows I love my daughter, but she doesn't know a thing that is useful. For her Christmas vac, as she calls it—and I think it lasts for forty days and forty nights—she wants to go on a sailing cruise in the Bermuda triangle. A crew of all girls, with a male skipper. If I were sure she would disappear . . ."

"He doesn't mean a word of it," Jane assured her guests, "and the cruise is in the Virgin Islands."

"Where only the islands can claim that name," said Alster sardonically.

His guests, even Jane, laughed aloud.

"It's just another of her ideas," Alster explained. "Something happened to that delightful child when she was twelve."

"It's called adolescence," murmured Jane.

Alster snorted.

"The young people of today are encouraged to have ideas," said Carolyn Hulverson.

"Crazy ones especially," said Margaret's father. "Why, Don, that girl can make all your patients sound rational."

"Some of 'em sound that way on their own."

"Yes, I know they do, but— I suppose hysteria would better describe some of the causes she espouses. We never know—kids these days can't write letters. They phone. Collect, of course."

"If she did write, she wouldn't say more than she does on the phone," Jane pointed out. "That she needs twenty-five dollars by Thursday."

"Yes, and if I ask her what for, she says I would not understand."

"They make that a catchall word over in the wards, too," Dr. Hulverson agreed.

"And if she comes home, without warning, and we eat over in the staff mess, what does that beautiful young girl do? When the waiter comes to serve us, she asks him to sit down and eat with us."

"He was more shocked than Alster was," Jane laughed.

Margaret's father nodded. "Yes, he was. I think I should have let the fellow sit in on her arguments. But it made no difference; that year it was equality for the minority groups. The last time she was home she was full of romantic ideas about living naturally. She wanted Jane and me to go around in bare feet and our bathrobes. Clothes were constricting—"

"Today would be a good one for that procedure," said Don. "How do you handle these things?"

"At first he swore," said Jane. "Then he tried listening to her."

"And if we brought up some idea she had been working on the last time she was at home, she would look at us as if we were crazy."

"I regret the bare feet, bathrobe project."

"Oh, the bathrobes were to serve only until she could get us some of the African duds she was wearing. You take a length of material, cut a hole in the middle, put it over your head, and you are clothed."

"Until the wind blows," laughed Jane, reaching for the ringing telephone.

Both doctors waited alertly. Jane held the phone out to her husband.

He came to stand beside the table, and spoke quietly

into the instrument. "Alster here."

Jane watched him closely; their guests pretended to be disinterested but of course were not. In their tight-knit community everyone's affairs concerned everyone.

"Yes," said the tall, dark man quietly. And *yes* again. Then there was a long silence.

"Oh, oh!" breathed Jane softly.

Alster listened still for a minute, or two, then he said, "I understand. Thank you."

And he sat the phone down, precisely. Not saying a word, he crossed to the small bar and poured himself a stiff drink.

"Bad news, eh?" said Don Hulverson.

Dr. Alster walked to the window and closed the draperies.

"Yes," he said tightly. "That was news that my contract is not going to be renewed. I am out of a job."

"Did they say . . . ?"

"They said I was free to go wherever I liked."

There was a frozen moment of silence.

"Did they— Do you have any idea of where that will be?" asked Carolyn.

"Well, I suppose it will be wherever a hospital will have me," said Alster. He turned and threw the glass he held into the fire. He was extremely angry, his face dead white, his lips and eyes slits of rage.

"We once had Waterford glasses," Jane said quietly.

Alster whirled on her, then turned away again. Before guests he would not further show his anger.

Carolyn stood up. "I think we had better get home, Papa," she said to Don.

"No hurry," said Alster grimly. "We won't start packing what's left of the glassware until after Christmas."

"Do you know . . . ?" Don asked him, helping Carolyn with her poncho.

"I can guess. They call it rule infraction. But—"

"Your cholesterol tests?"

"Yes."

"What's that all about?" asked Jane alertly.

The men barely glanced at her. "I suppose some newspaper got word . . ."

"The men talk to their families, and families chatter like magpies—and there you have it. We are using the veterans as guinea pigs."

"Are you?" Jane asked hardily.

Both men ignored her. "But this was the hospital . . ."

"Yes. Where PAS was tested and proven," Alster agreed with Hulverson. "Yes, it was. And now we don't see one case of TB in a year."

"That was before Nader and his friends, too."

"Yes. And the smarty college kids who can't write or read, but do bleed for the veterans being cared for by the government."

Jane stepped between the two men. "If you are not going to tell us what this is all about . . ." she said threateningly.

Don shrugged into his coat. "He'll tell you," he promised. "But I think he'll do it better without Carolyn and me around. Good-bye, sweetie, and thanks for the drink." He stooped and kissed her cheek. "Be seein' you, Doc," he said as he passed Alster.

Alster made a sound of some sort. He was putting fresh wood on the fire. When he straightened, it was to be confronted by his wife. There was no evading her.

Jane Alster was a pretty woman, with ash-blond hair that waved softly back from her face. She had beautiful eyes and was tall enough so that her husband could not ignore her presence, nor her demands.

"All right, all right," he said, "though I thought I would do rounds while you fixed us some dinner."

"You won't do rounds smelling of six ounces of Wild Turkey," she reminded him.

"What difference would it make now?"

"The difference is that we would begin packing tomorrow."

He nodded. "You may be right," he agreed.

"Alster . . ."

"All right, all right. If I don't talk, you'll nag me."

"I have every right to nag you."

"Perhaps you do. Well, sit down, and I'll give you a lecture on institutional doctoring."

"Spare me," said Jane, sitting down again behind her table of grasses and fruits of the field. "I know you are a good doctor, that you get bored with a hospital and its institutionalized patients. That you would like to be able to do research and special surgery."

Alster leaned back in his chair, and reached for a magazine.

"Why were you fired?" asked Jane, her tone brightly interested. "It wasn't a woman and her charges. You spoke of tests to Hulverson. What tests?"

"Cholesterol tests," said Alster. "Do you know what cholesterol is?"

"Oh, yes. TV and the media keep us well informed."

"All right, then. Do you understand that we have to have cholesterol in our bodies, in our food, or we would dry up like one of those leaves out on the lawn?"

"They are not dry tonight."

"No, they are not. But my concern, my research, has been in what causes some people to build up artery-closing cholesterol and others not to. Supposedly our diet is behind it. Though Eskimos live on fat and almost never have high blood pressure or heart attacks. Japanese live on fish and do have those things. Yet when the Japanese come to this country and live on our sort of food, often the BP is less bothersome. Why?"

"I'm sure you will tell me."

"I won't, because I don't know. But, some months ago, we got a nut in here who insisted on a vegetarian diet, and he said it was to avoid the cholesterol. I didn't agree with all the theories he had—he was a real nut! But I thought I would like to find out if vegetarians were on a better track than the carnivores."

"Of which you are really a member."

"Yes, I am. I like my steaks marbled, and my lamb chops with a crispy edge of fat. But to go back to the tests."

"Were they authorized?"

"No, they were not."

"And they should have been?"

"I suppose. They call such research risky experimentation."

"But you did it, anyway, when you should have known better." Her voice was smooth, and maddeningly cool.

"Well, damn it, Jane!"

"You know the position the boards have had to take!"

"Yes, I know it, but I wasn't doing experimental lobotomies or anything like that. I was doing a perfectly harmless experiment. A survey. It was good research and could do harm to no one."

"It seems to have harmed you."

Alster growled and sank further into his chair. "Go fix dinner," he said grouchily.

"Did it get into the paper?"

"It must have. Maybe someone wrote a letter. Or talked out of turn. The diet kitchen doesn't like special orders. They get menus made up in Washington or somewhere, and they want to stick to them. And, by God, they do stick to them! You see plates full of carrots going back to the kitchen after every dinner. And the next morning you see huge bags of carrots coming up the ramp to the kitchen."

Jane got up from her chair and came over to him. "Tell me about it," she urged.

"Don't you dare rub your fingers through my hair!"

She laughed. "I never have, but now that you mention it—"

"Jane!"

"I won't, I won't," she promised. "But tell me what you did. It had to do with diet, I gather."

"Yes, it did. I worked with the meat versus vegetable theories."

"Results?"

"Oh, yes."

"Tell me."

"Well, I've been doing it for only a few months. I first selected thirty men who were in good, average health. And they were put on a high-protein diet. Meat, at least one egg a day, what most Americans would call a regular diet. Then I selected thirty more—healthy, and some of them quite rational. I explained that I was doing an experiment—"

"Oh, oh!"

"Yes. I should not have said the dirty word. But I did, and they agreed to live on a strictly vegetable diet. Margarine, vegetables, fruits. No fats or animal products."

"And the diet kitchen raised a fuss."

"Not really. I am medical officer and if I say that

thirty patients on various wards should have a vegetable diet, they get it."

"And you made regular tests for cholesterol."

"Yes, I did. And at the end—you may not believe this, Jane. Most of the medics found it hard to believe. At the end of a month, there was absolutely no change in the cholesterol count. Diet had made no difference."

"And you published this."

"I told the staff."

"And . . . ?"

"Someone said I hadn't done it long enough. I agreed. So I continued it for three months."

"And—"

"There was no difference. Now this was an important finding, Jane."

"It sounds that way to me."

"But where I made my mistake was to call the head man in Washington."

"Did he wash you out?"

"No, but he had to file my report. He did tell me that I should remember I had been a military man and should know when to retreat, and how."

"And you stopped your experiments."

"I am military man enough to know how to obey orders."

"Yes. But it's too bad, if you were getting significant results. Maybe you should write a paper of your own."

"I'll wait and see if there is a chance for me to get a government job elsewhere."

"That would be prudent. But I am proud of your experiment."

"I did get results," Alster mused. "There was just one thing I have not been able to figure out, and that is why the fellows on the vegetarian diet excrete more fat than the meat eaters."

She stared at him, then she laughed. "I think the comment on that is, 'Hush up, Dr. Alster!'"

He laughed and picked up his magazine. Jane decided that it was time for her to fix dinner.

After they had eaten, on the card table, which she had cleared by pitching all her dried weeds into the fire: "I am not going to do any holiday decoration for this dump," she declared. She had spread a gold-colored cloth, set it with brown pottery and served a tasty mixture of wine sauce, sliced eggs, crab meat, and green peppers on rounds of English muffins.

After they had eaten, she asked Alster where they would go now. What work would they do?

"I have three months to decide," he told her.

"Two."

"No, the contracts are signed at the end of the month in which they come up, so I have January if I want to use it."

"I see. Well?"

"You do nag, my darling."

"Mmmm. And you have rounds to make. But give me some sort of answer."

"I can't think why I ever married you."

"Well, I remember exactly. So answer me, if only to say that you don't know what you will do next."

"If that will satisfy you—"

"It won't."

"All right, then." He glanced at his watch. "I have had an offer to be medical officer at an industrial center."

"Oh, no!"

"Not a plant doctor, Jane. This is one of those big complexes the conglomerates build. A factory that looks like a resort hotel. Houses and swimming pools and camellia bushes for the help. And a hospital for the employees *and* their families."

"Gee," said Jane, rising to clear the table. Then she turned. "Camellias?" she asked.

"It's in California."

She frowned.

"Not the southern part. Up north of San Francisco."

The frown smoothed away.

"It's a big operation—a wood-products concern; they make everything from board lumber to salad bowls and milk cartons."

She looked dubious. "Milk cartons made of wood?"

"Your evening newspaper is made out of wood, my dear."

"Yes, I suppose. When did you get this offer?"

"Some time ago. Six weeks, perhaps. But I was into my research thing, and satisfied with the lovely climate here."

"Could you . . . ?"

"Yes, I could. I could continue the research. I'd need to establish new guinea pigs, of course. But I've kept records on the work here. I never did use names; they are numbers. I have copies of these records, and they will be a big help if I ever start the thing again."

"As you will."

"I suppose." He went to the closet for his coat.

"Why . . ." said Jane, coming in from the kitchen. "I know that you never discuss things that are of the utmost importance to me. But why and when did you get this offer of a job in a milk-carton factory?"

He chuckled. "I had a letter a few weeks ago. The position may have been filled by now. But the consultant surgeon there knew me, and he thought I might be interested."

"Were you? At the time, I mean."

"Well, yes, somewhat. It sounded more attractive weatherwise."

She lifted the long spoon she held.

He put up a protective hand. "If what we are getting outside tonight cannot be called weatherwise, what could be?"

"I think you're right. But the situation sounded attractive."

"But I knew you would throw a triple fit at the idea of leaving."

"I've learned to be expert. And I also have learned that my fits do me no good."

"That's right. So, well, and anyway—briefly, too—this town—it really is that—is in the lumbering country, which means the beautiful forests of northern California. You've been through there. Dunkirk—all that. No! It isn't at Dunkirk. It has its own name, which is Indian, and escapes me at the moment. But they do logging, they make plywood—they grind pulp; some of it they glue together and make fiberboard. Wallboard. Fertilizer. Wood chips for flower beds—oh, hundreds of things."

"And they have a hospital."

"Yes, they do. Not too large. Forty-five beds, I think. Because of the workers' families, and those of the executives, too. They provide houses and schools and shops for their people. They provide entertainment—from tennis courts to puppet shows. Swimming. And a house would be available to me. To us."

"What sort of house?"

"The letter said an oddball house."

"Now what was that supposed to mean?"

"There was an addendum—'oddball,' like me. In other words, not the cheesebox that we have here."

She put the spoon down. Her eyes narrowed. She

moved toward Alster. "Who was the surgeon who wrote you?" she asked tensely.

"Oh, a guy. I've known a lot of surgeons. And it would not surprise me at all to know that most of them consider me to be an oddball." He went to the front door.

"Alster!"

He stopped, looked over his shoulder.

"Don't touch that doorknob," she said.

He dropped his hand. "Well, it happened to be Murphy Anderson," he said casually, and he put his hand again on the doorknob.

She sprang at him. "Six weeks ago!" she screamed. "You had a letter from *Murphy Anderson* and you didn't tell me? He offered you a job and you didn't tell me? You've been considering California, and *you didn't tell me?*" Her voice rose, and rose.

He waited. He knew Jane. As it was, the whole area knew that she was making a scene. Tomorrow they would guess why. But if he left, she would follow him, and—

He unbuttoned his heavy coat, went over to his chair and sat down. He would wait.

Finally she began to talk. Not rationally, exactly. He looked at his watch. He really should make rounds. Bed check.

"I'll agree," said Jane breathlessly; her hair was atumble about her face and her cheeks were crimson. "I'll agree that you know Murphy and that he knows you. I'll agree that he can wrap you around his finger. Why does he want you out in California? There has to be a reason. Doesn't he want that job himself?"

"He doesn't live or work at the complex. He lives near and is on a hospital staff in a fairly large town down the mountain—or perhaps it's up the mountain.

But he said that this was a good job, with all sorts of advantages."

"He's using you. Or wants to."

"I can take care of myself." He stood up and buttoned his coat.

He went out through the door this time, hearing Jane's last words. She knew exactly how well he could take care of himself! Indeed she did! Alster sighed.

The next morning she sought Alster in his office at the hospital. She was popular with the patients and was often to be seen on the wards. But she did not often come to her husband's office. She was knowledgeable about hospital etiquette and protocol. But that morning—

"You said last night . . ." she spoke quietly, without any further preliminaries than a "good morning" to his secretary. She closed the inner door behind the woman.

"Tell me," she began again. "Has Murphy been holding the job he wants you to take?"

"He told me only that such a job would be open."

"That he had held it?"

"He said he was going into private practice and staff work."

"Up the ladder, of course. You are sure he won't be your boss?"

"I don't think so. This job is that of 'surgeon in charge.' Medical office of the complex hospital. I'd be accountable to local medical authorities, and to the complex's board."

"Not Murphy."

"I am sure not Murphy. I don't know his precise plans."

"Just as you don't know yours."

"Look, Jane, I am sorry we have to move. But suppose we deal with ourselves, with our own problems. That should be enough. Murphy doesn't need, and probably doesn't want, our advice. He sent me this letter in good faith . . ."

"And you have decided to accept his offer."

"It sounds promising." He buzzed for his secretary and asked for the Dr. Anderson file. Correspondence. He gave this to Jane. "There are pictures of the surrounding country . . ."

"I think you are accepting Murphy's offer to vex me."

"I hadn't considered that idea. I was thinking about the salary I'll get, and the cost of moving to California. The trouble."

She was looking at brochures, clippings from magazines, reading Murphy's short letter. "The wooded mountains are beautiful," she said.

"Square dancing every Saturday night."

She ignored him. "Is it near the ocean?"

"Not really. A hundred miles, I should judge. There's a river. And good roads."

"Is this the oddball house?" she asked, holding one picture toward him.

"I suspect it is. A creative architectural experiment, it is called. The main offices look damned experimental to me, too. Open trusses, clerestory lighting."

"What's the hospital like?"

"It's in there, somewhere. Very modern."

She nodded. "Have you called Murph?"

"It's still breakfast time out there."

"But you are going to . . ."

"I have a few questions. But the medical aspect has to be important, Jane."

"I know that. Glory be, I should know it by now. Margaret will change schools."

"She might."

"She will. Because of transportation costs, if nothing else."

"There will be all sorts of costs."

"Do you plan to leave before the first of the year?"

"If a replacement for me were available, and we could be packed and ready."

"Mmmm. My Christmas gift will be a receipted bill from the movers."

"Oh, now look, Jane! I'll not take this place unless there are certain concessions."

"Moving bills?"

"That could happen. I was thinking of retirement benefits, family insurance— And once we are out there, it will certainly be cheaper to live in the suburbs. That map shows the complex built right along the bank of a river, which must be sizable because it used to be the means of getting logs to the ocean port or to some sawmill."

"And you would get up early every morning to catch your kippers for breakfast."

He laughed. "But I might. And you might, too. It's possible that we both could go rustic and enjoy it. The climate is mild . . ."

"It's mild here, some of the time."

"Yes, it is, and this is a pretty location. But I am not able to stay here." His voice went icy.

"I know," she conceded. "I'm sorry I feel as I do. But the whole thing has been a shock to me."

"And to me. But I have had a little time to think about the California thing."

"And going rustic." She laughed. "I can just see you. But you are right. There are forests close, and there will be fishing. Skiing, do you suppose? I am thinking of Margaret, not me."

"There certainly would be skiing a lot closer than

where we are now. And probably other recreation possibilities. These big projects have to hold, and entertain, their employees, both white collar and blue."

She sat thoughtful, sliding the papers on her lap, glancing at them. "Would you have a chance, freedom and time, to build up a private practice?"

"Why should I?"

"What's good for Murph should be good for you."

"I see. We really don't know much about what Murphy is doing."

"No, we don't. Was he ever, do you suppose, in the job he wants you to take?"

"I don't know. We don't correspond. Offhand, I'd say he may have helped organize the medical service for the complex."

"Yes, that sounds like him. But when you talk to him, ask him about the private practice possibilities."

He made a note on his memo pad. "I'll tell you tonight what he has to say."

"Could I stick around now? While you call?"

"No, you could not. He would suspect you were here, if you did as much as breathe."

"Mmmm. He would." But she still did not rise.

Dr. Alster looked at his watch. The corners of her mouth lifted. She knew that he wanted her to leave. "I was wondering," she said slowly, "since you do have time, if perhaps you could talk to Mike . . ."

Mike was Alster's son by his first marriage, a seminarian about to be ordained to the ministry of the Episcopal Church. Their relationship was good, though they saw little of each other.

"I don't think so," Mike's father told Jane. "For the first thing, few children understand, or comprehend exactly, what the father does for a living. To Mike, I am a doctor, and that is all."

"He's a smart fellow."

"Yes, he is. And he would try to help me if I needed help."

"But you don't."

"Not if the California job is still open. In any case, I have to go somewhere. I must work. You know that."

She knew that he must. She knew Alster as well as a wife ever knows a man. Her husband was a good doctor. He was well educated, he kept up, and he did good work. She once had been a nurse working under him, and she knew these things for facts. He was a keen diagnostician; he was a skillful surgeon, and his interest in a case did not die when he stripped off his gloves after surgery—as happened too often with doctors these days. She knew that too well. He would see a compound fracture through healing and therapy to maximum cure. He could tell a real illness, masked by what looked like the depression of old age. He could be harsh and give harsh orders to a malingering veteran here in this hospital; she had seen him as gentle as a woman with one who was frightened or in excruciating pain. She knew these things, just as she knew about the bottle he kept in a locked drawer of his desk. The whole hospital probably knew about that bottle. How Dr. Alster could walk swiftly down the corridor, turn in at his office, lock the door behind him, and within minutes come out again with the fine aura of bourbon about him.

She began to gather the papers in her lap. "It says here that the hospital has thirty-five beds."

"I know it does. Murphy said forty-five."

"You've talked to him?"

"About a month ago. A follow-up on the letter."

"What else did he tell you?"

"Not much. That the hospital was small, well

equipped. That it cared for the families of the employees as well as the workers."

"Would you work alone?"

"Oh, no! He said there was a house doctor."

"Meaning . . . ?"

"He didn't elaborate, Jane. But I gathered he meant someone with the status of resident doctor."

"Young."

"Probably. And he also mentioned consultant help when required."

"Murphy himself."

"Probably. Now if you will please get the hell out of here? I want to make that call, and I have some surgery at eleven."

Baumgarten. Alster said it meant tree garden, but Jane had paid small attention to that; she thought it a strange name for a suburb.

"No doubt they will change it for you," said Alster, rising to be sure she left.

2

If Baumgarten did mean tree garden, the name was apt. The town was a pretty one, built along the bank of the river, which separated the suburb from the main city of Scott. The rushing river; the great wooded hills rising and rising again—and there, surrounding the reflecting basin called the pond, the glass walls of the complex buildings. Factory, warehouses, offices, the hospital. Windows and windows and windows. The wood used was cedar, weathered to a soft, furry grey.

Above and around the angled buildings of the complex, the clustered houses rising with them, were the woods. The forests. Tall trees, thick with shade, hundreds and hundreds of trees. Chimneys appeared here and there; a broad street swept upward and disappeared among the trees. The glass window-walls of the business buildings reflected the sky and repeated the woods in their mirrors. The forests. There were flowers, and patches of lawn, a fountain in a courtyard—and the river, which ran swiftly and shouted its song. The first floor of the main building of the great complex was below street level; its windows and lights and its people reflected in the pond, which was like a glass mirror. This pond was at the rear of the building, with a long window wall facing it and the wooded hillside.

The busy office structure started below street level, but the windows captured and repeated the sylvan setting. Within, one could see small conference rooms, unadorned, functional; the lighting was the industrial-warehouse type, ducts were exposed and painted red. The main factory building and its entrance was on the higher level and, like all the buildings of the complex, was built of cedar. The interiors were open to view, with the truss supports left exposed. The work or office cubicles on the lower level faced the pond; the luxuries embodied in all the buildings—office, warehouse, factory, and hospital—were the height of the ceilings and the view. Here the complex and the work it did were the important things. The people who moved about and were busy faded into insignificance.

The hospital, too, had this appearance of openness and strength, though there must be concealed rooms. The homes were open trussed, wide windowed, with color glowing from within.

When Joe Raithel had first come to work at the complex, he thought he could never endure the openness, the lack of privacy. Within days he realized that, with everyone working, as it were, in the open woods, there was less concern about what could be seen and what was being done than there had been in the big hospital where he had trained. There no windows had looked outward; the place was a mighty layer after layer of floors, raised on a mighty forklift; and because they did not know what went on behind all the doors and the curtains, there was curiosity and surmise. Here, Joe knew what he was doing. The patients knew; their friends, seeing them through a window, knew that the blond, serious-faced young doctor was taking care of those who needed care. Binding a cut hand, giving a shot in the arm, listening with a stethoscope—what was so unusual about that? Why look? There were better things to do.

At first, Joe himself had been apprehensive. There were, the head nurse told him, "bedpan draperies" that he could use. And he did use them, gradually forgetting that they were there. The hospital building was off the main street, and the ground squirrels and mountain jays didn't seem to care about what the doctor was doing. Dr. Anderson had taken him through the first months at the hospital, but now Joe was on his own and this frightened him, though he felt sure he should not show that he was frightened. This independence was temporary, he realized. He wished he could take it on alone, the medical service for the complex workers and their families, just as he wished he need not go on living with his mother over in Scott. Of course, living there, Joe's being a local "boy" had given him a boost in getting this job, but somehow he knew that if he had an apartment of his own, or one of the town houses built up on the mountainside, he would feel more of a man. His mother said the place would be a mess, and it might be. Or Joe, on his own, possibly would hang up his clothes, pick up the newspapers, leave the place neat, and his own, free to go down the hill to his office and the medical work he would do on his own, too.

He loved his mother, but her attendance on him often was oppressive. She questioned him, she watched him; she called it loving him, and loving no doubt it was. Though Joe was not an only child. He had a sister married to an Army man and living overseas. A brother, and his brother's family, lived down the coast, three hundred miles away, or near, as one chose to consider it.

When he knew that Dr. Anderson was leaving, Joe

considered seeking a place somewhere away from Scott and Baumgarten. Trained doctors were at a premium, he could find a place in the Midwest, or almost anywhere.

But his mother would guess why he was leaving. Something had happened, she would say. Dr. Anderson had done something that forced the company to dismiss him, and out of loyalty Joe felt that he must go too. She would build up quite a story, as she so often did; and then, having woven it in her own mind, she would begin gradually to reveal the fabric of it. . . .

No. It was much simpler to stay on here, live with his mother, and wonder what the new head doctor would be like.

But he did wish he had not really been endowed with a conscience that kept him close enough to his mother to feel, constantly, the warmth of her brooding feathers and wings.

If his brother had not been in poor health, perhaps he could have made the break. If Charles and his family could, somewhat regularly, come up to Scott for the weekend—but Charles was not well, and Joe's main effort, one of his efforts, was to resist his mother's wish to go down there and visit *him*. Sometimes they did go—a half-dozen times a year—and Joe insisted that they stay in a motel, or make the trip all in one day. Seeing Charles was his mother's right, and Joe himself was interested in the health and abilities of his brother.

This thing he did for his mother— Oh, he did many things for her, of course. But the situation was difficult. He had almost persuaded her that she must not come over to Baumgarten and "drop in ' at the hospital or his office. The personnel was lovely to Mrs. Raithel.

But she talked to them, and she spoke for Joe on too many subjects. This could be embarrassing, if not worse. "Joe likes dark-haired girls better than he does blondes," she had been known to say. Even Dr. Anderson had joked about that. And it was only a joke. But when she told them that Joe thought the measles vaccine a waste of time and money—*that* caused some trouble. The children of the employees should have their immunizations, and what did his mother know about it, anyway? Certainly she had no way of knowing what Joe thought! He had to be firm with her about such matters, and he was going to have to be firm with her about Charles. Already Mrs. Raithel was making elaborate plans for the whole family to vacation together during the next summer. Charles and his wife and two kids, Joe and their mother . . .

Charles was not able to spend two weeks on the beach, or maybe in one of two campers in Yosemite. Charles was ill. He was seriously ill, and Joe had tried to convey that fact to their mother without actually telling her how sick the man was. If he did convince her, she would immediately move in on poor Charles—or she would want him brought to Scott, where Joe could "doctor" him. He could not persuade his mother that he still was in the learning stage of medicine. "But I'll be here to help you," she would say. "Goodness, I took care of you three children from the time you were born. I know Charles can't eat certain things—I could help."

So he did not tell her that Charles was very sick. A cop out, and he knew it.

And into this beautiful paradise, which already had its apple tree and its serpent, as well as Adam and Eve and their family, came Jane Alster. She was to "look the place over," find a home for herself and the new doctor in charge. There was a house. The one Murphy called "oddball." But it might be too oddball, even for the Alsters. And the thing was furnished, but if the Alsters wanted to bring their own furniture, or some of it . . . the best thing had seemed to be to have Jane make a quick flight to California and look at the oddball house, its furnishings, probably also oddball.

So there she was, looking smart in a creamy camel's hair coat and a mink hat that hugged her head—indeed it seemed to have grown there. She was met by a pleasant young woman from the "office," taken first to the guesthouse where she would stay for a day or two. She had an eye-opening view of the complex, the pond, the wooded mountainside; reflected and repeated in a dozen ways. And she saw the house that was long, that looked narrow but was not. Its walls, grey cedar and glass, sloped upward and inward to the row of clerestory windows and the roof. On the street side, that was. Within, there was a feeling of space, and quiet, and rest. The furniture was deep, and comfortable, and functional. There was a beautiful kitchen and dining area, with topiary trees and hanging baskets. Open-back stairs to the bedrooms circled upward in the center of the house, with a landing on which stood a grand piano. A large triangle of the lower floor was marked off by thick green carpeting, deep window seats that were couches. Other couches faced the two-story-high windows. There was a square fireplace tiled in green, the hearth raised above the floor. And again there were growing plants—and the soft carpet, the seclusion, the deep green couches, the tall, tall windows that brought in the green of the out-of-doors, reflected and seen again in the waters of the pond.

The Alster furniture would definitely not do. They would store it and move in here. If only to see Alster's face when first he saw his new home. The bedrooms overlooked the lower floor, and there were angled walls, but no doors.

"Like the rest-rooms at the Kansas City airport," said Jane to her guide. "I wandered into the men's room there one time. Very interesting."

Her guide smiled.

"Did Murphy Anderson live here?" asked Jane.

"Dr. Anderson? Oh, no. He lived in one of the hill cottages. Now he lives in Scott. There's a child, you know?"

Jane knew.

Jane was expected at a small dinner, to be held in what was called the club dining room, that evening at six. No one would dress.

"And they'll look me over?"

"Yes, and you will meet the executive officers and their wives. You can think about the house and tell us tomorrow."

She would think about the officers, too. She had already decided about the house. What *would* Alster find to say? The clerestory windows, the trusses, and the open walls. The window wall that brought the pond and the woods into the house. Well, of course he would adjust, just as he had to the stucco duplex in Missouri, and the adobe in New Mexico. Wordily, but he would adjust. The people— There Jane must consider herself, as well as Alster. Though, of course, Alster—

She had brought what she hoped would be a proper dress for the dinner. She brushed her blond hair into a shining cap, with little curling locks escaping before her ears and on the nape of her neck. The dress was a dull rose, extremely simple, but with a *concha* belt and silver slippers to match it. The belt was always a conversation starter.

And, as always, she liked the men better than the

women. And this worked somewhat in reverse. She talked about the belt, and Alster. She talked about Sangria jelly she had made—this for the ladies—and she studied everyone. And to each one she talked about Alster.

The people were types. She had encountered them all before in the various places where Alster had worked, and Jane had lived, in the past seventeen years.

The club, of course, featured wood—the walls were either glass or of barn siding, waxed and rubbed. The tables were butcher blocks on which the linen and glass and china looked beautiful. Jane was surprised and said so. That, also, was a conversation piece.

The men—she looked them over, and there were all the types. Beside her the fortyish fellow, with curly blond hair receding from his forehead, camel's hair jacket and brown velvet vest. General manager or something. There were youthful-looking men with open-collared, patterned shirts; a charmer in a turtle-neck; and the solid citizen in a blue, vested suit, a well-fitting shirt collar and a pretty good tie . . .

And then there were the women. The guide of the afternoon was not there. But the center of the group, the leader— Jane could like that woman, and the men certainly did. She had dark hair, she was thin, with a rough skin and mottled legs, yet she wore her clothes with style. She had a hearty laugh and matched the men in the jokes she told. There was the couple—the man drank too much, his wife tried to prevent this and he left the table, went to the bar, and triumphantly brought back a double martini. There was a small, kitten-faced woman who wore a turbaned hat, and seemed demure but, if given the chance, talked endlessly. She was in the public relations department.

There were wives who were wives and held no office in the plant.

"I'll come to know them all, and too well," Jane told herself.

Yes, she said, she did like the house. The kitchen was a marvel—she would entertain there—and, of course, the living room, the carpet, the velvet couches—

Would Dr. Alster like it?

"Well, let me tell you about Dr. A." And she did tell.

Of course he was a good doctor, she said. Of course he was good looking. They were lucky to get him. He was one of a vanishing species, skilled, up to date, yet with the old-time compassion and interest for his patients. He had many interests; he did research . . .

"It sounds like the second coming to me," drawled the turbaned little woman who was in public relations. "And Jane here is his prophet." She spoke just loudly enough for Jane to hear.

She did not flick an eyelash. She leaned forward to speak to the solemn-faced young man who sat across from her. He was the junior doctor at the hospital.

"I am counting on your showing me through the hospital tomorrow," she told him. "Alster will want to know so many things."

Joe Raithel was awed. He surely would show Mrs. Alster what they had. They set a time and Jane turned, smiling, to the man beside her.

She wanted to see everything, she said.

The next day they showed her "everything." Again she had her guide, who evidently had had a report on the dinner party. She showed Jane the charming nondenominational chapel, which, again, brought the out-of-doors inside by means of a wide, clear window behind the altar. Jane had seen the clubhouse; she spent some time in the "newspaper" office, which really was one. It had wire service, and it sent regular issues out to the offices across the country, to the men in the logging camps—an upward and backward jerk of the head indicated the mountains.

Jane would *love* to see a logging camp. So she did see one, and ate her noon meal with the men, complimenting the cook.

"I'd swear you didn't eat sourdough and slabs of beef every day," said that cook, a woman as wide as she was tall, with cheeks like red apples, and a tennis hat on the back of her head.

"Would you drive a little farther up into the woods?" Jane asked her guide.

"If that's what you want."

It evidently was what Jane wanted, for she waxed lyrical over the tall trees, the smell of the pines. "There must be fish in those swift streams," she told the guide.

The young woman nodded. "There are fish. But don't plan to canoe or wade the rivers. They come down from glaciers."

"I'll remember. Now, could I walk just a little way into the woods, and sense the quiet?"

She could. Later the guide told her fellow workers, "I don't know if she's real or a phony," she said. "She seems to *feel* things."

"Everything is new to her. We are used to it," one of the men pointed out.

"I'm real anxious to see that there Alster," drawled the guide.

The employees, the town, looked at Jane Alster and watched her. She was going to stay a third day. "To measure things," she explained. She went to the hospital and laughed about the "bed-pan curtains." She said that she had trained to be a nurse, but had married so young. She looked at and saw everything in the hospital, and Joe Raithel told her that he was going to take her to his home to have dinner with his mother. He did not mention how much argument had been involved in that invitation. But Jane may have guessed. She put on a fresh blouse and went with Joe, across the bridge to Scott, which her alert eyes examined, too. Shopping mall, public park, small airfield, pleasant homes, row houses, and apartment complexes. Nowhere did she meet up with Murphy. She had expected to see him.

Mrs. Raithel was as much of a type as was Joe, the earnest, anxious young doctor, with his smooth blond hair and his hesitant way of talking about himself. In the hospital, on medical subjects, he was more articulate.

Jane concentrated on the mother. Could she help get dinner on the table? Mrs. Raithel said she had not "fixed" much. If Joe had given her a little notice . . .

"Everything looks fine," said Jane. Salmon steaks, baked potatoes, a lettuce and tomato salad. Jane encouraged Joe's mother to talk about her family: a daughter, married; and another son. He lived down the coast but was not in good health.

"He has leukemia," said Joe quietly.

Jane's glance showed that she understood what was involved.

"One doctor told me it was aplastic anemia," said Mrs. Raithel.

"It is leukemia," declared Joe.

"Is he hospitalized?" Jane asked.

"In and out. I help as I can."

"I'm sure you do."

She was charming and Joe, at least, was charmed. Jane said he must tell her all about his brother when they moved to the complex in January.

"You really are coming, then?" asked Joe.

"Oh, yes. It's to be Alster's job. I came out to look at places where we might live."

"Do you like the display house?"

"Is that what it is? There are houses up the mountainside, and I understand many of the employees live on this side of the river."

"They do. There are buses. Have you looked at other places?"

"No. I am intrigued with the display house. I didn't know that was what it was."

"They let an architect build his idea of what wood could do."

"And he did. It is a fascinating place."

Had Mrs. Raithel seen it?

She had. "I like things more snug," she said.

"I know what you mean," said Jane.

"I'm glad you are coming," Joe told her. "The architect thought there should be a small pool at the foot of the steps to the west, right into the woods."

"But there should be!" cried Jane. "Alster would love just such a pool."

At noon the next day she said this to the assembled executives. Except for some wives, these were largely the same people she had met at dinner. She again wore the mink cap and her good suit. She said she was delighted with the location of Alster's new position. "He will love the woods, and he'll quote Thoreau to you about gaining as much from contemplating nature as one does from building a fence or digging a ditch."

"Don't say that to these people," cried the man beside her, feigning alarm. "They will all leave their desks—"

"I thought I knew my Thoreau . . ." said the public relations woman.

"Oh, then you and Alster should have quotation swappings," said Jane. "This particular one had to do with building a fence. Alster could quote it exactly. It says something about one's neighbors admiring a man who would work diligently and hard for three weeks, digging the foundation for a stone fence, and would call him an industrious fellow. Yet, if that same man devoted himself to something of real value, but would bring in little money, they might be inclined to call him an idle loafer." She smiled enchantingly at her audience. "Don't be quick to call Alster a loafer. And don't be bored when he quotes Thoreau, either. Such things are his hobby. He'll do much for you because he will wander up the path to the trees. Of course, he can bore you on the subject, as I am afraid I may have done."

Someone asked her about the house. Did she really think they could live there?

"Of course! It is just right for us. Murphy said it would be oddball, and it is! But let Alster have his swimming pool, and let me find a small corner for a table, a chair, my typewriter, and my books— I do a little writing, you know."

They did not know. Excited, they questioned her, and, excited, she answered. That was why the location must be just right! "It is important to both of us. It will be important to the family when they visit."

But she had not told them about the family!

She glanced at her watch. But of course she did have a family. They did. There was a son. Alster's son, actually. Ready to be ordained as a clergyman in the Episcopal Church, but very young and most interesting. And there was their daughter. "She belongs to both of us. She's in school, of course. Sixteen, such an enchanting and infuriating age!"

Jane was charming them all. "We are getting quite a bonus in this Alster fella," said Hilda Curren when the meeting broke up because Jane must catch her plane. "Let me drive her in. I could have an article for the *Organ*."

So she always referred to the company newspaper, issued once a week. "Maybe she'll write me out of a job."

"Don't count on it," said Kate Beetz in her blunt, hearty way. "Coming in here an hour ago, she gushed over what she called the blowing bamboo trees."

Six people turned to stare at her. "That clump of willows outside the dispatch office," said Kate.

"Did you tell her?" asked Hilda.

"Certainly I told her," said Kate, "and she did not like it. She does not like to make mistakes, and she showed it. So watch your step, Hilda. Don't let her stub her toe again. She'll blame you, not herself."

Afterward, of course, everyone talked about Jane Alster. The attendant in the powder room at the club, the members who had had dinner with her as they had dinner with each other almost every Friday night. Husbands talked to wives, and wives talked to each other. The town itself talked. A new doctor in their hospital affected everyone in Baumgarten, and a few who lived in Scott, notably the Raithels. These people were the ones whom the Alsters would know, who would be their friends, or at least their associates.

Kate Beetz said they were in for some lively times. The men had liked Jane, the women decided upon a wait-and-see attitude. Would she and her "Alster" be members of their dinner group?

"He may prefer wandering off into the woods," drawled Helen Cobb.

"Oh, give them a chance!" said the men. "Murphy says he is what we need."

"And Alan likes him," said Anne Hother, who taught in the school.

"Alan?" asked someone. "Does he know the Alsters?"

"If Murphy knows them, Alan is bound to."

"Well, he's none too reliable," said Alice Denby.

"He knows whom he likes," Anne retorted.

"Poor kid."

"Not so poor to have Murphy back of him."

"Was he the reason Murphy went into private practice over in Scott?"

"Well, Alan can be destructive. And big corporations suffer from atrophy of the heart."

So Alan had been the reason. "We all liked Dr. Anderson," mourned Hilda Curren.

"We'll like the new man. Forget the impression Janie made, give the doctor a chance."

"Eric Pemscot says she is a bright, clever woman," said Kate Beetz, "and very pretty."

The women looked at each other. "So there you are," said Hilda.

The boss had spoken. Jane Alster would be accepted as graciously as possible.

During her three days in Baumgarten, Jane had expected to see Murphy Anderson. But she did not until she was ready to leave for the airport and home. She found him seated in his car outside the guesthouse; he got out, put her bag into the back seat, and went back to sit beside her. He was, he said, going to drive her to the main airport. He could do it in the time it would take for her to use the feeder-line plane and fly there. He wanted to see her . . .

"I've been expecting to see you," she said.

"I'm a working doctor. Did things go all right?"

"For me, or for them?" she asked, settling into the seat.

"Both, I think. I understand you are going to put Alster into that house."

"He'll like it."

"Who knows what Alster will like? The people here, the town—"

"I did fine, Murphy," she told him. "I think they were satisfied."

"Good. Let's keep it that way. I admit I was a bit surprised that Alster sent you. Whom did you meet? What did you see?"

She told him, and tried to remember the people's names. But evidently he knew exactly who had seen her. He mentioned the various ones. They were a cliquish set, he said. "Try to be in rather than out, Jane."

"So I have to *try?*"

"It will help Alster."

Yes, it would. And, as they drove along, he spoke briefly of the people she had met. He laughed when she said she had had dinner with Joe Raithel's mother. "Don't let the guy fall in love with you," he cautioned. "He's vulnerable. That mother of his, and his youth. Though he's a capable medic."

"I was nice to him. He talked to me about his brother."

"He talks to everybody about his brother. He won't accept the fact that the fellow cannot get well. He knows better, but he won't face what he knows. I suppose you met Kate Beetz."

"Oh, yes, indeed. She seems very popular."

"She's a smart woman, and good company. Widow, and wants no part of another husband. But when it comes to insurance actuaries, she wrote the book."

"The other men liked her, too. I could tell. So, of course, the women have to like her."

"Jane," he said warningly.

"All right, all right. Kate Beetz is great. Then there was this couple, the man drinks too much—"

"The Cobbs. And he does drink too much at parties. He's the head accountant."

"His wife . . ."

"She works, too, and she can get some screwy ideas. They have one child who—as the phrase used to go—had to be married at sixteen. Since then she has produced three of the damnedest kids you ever saw. Husband has left her and that's a break. But the Cobbs support the family; the daughter is supposed to keep house for them. They live in Baumgarten, bought an old apartment house. D'you meet the Jekels?"

"I did if he's the judge."

"He may have been a judge at one time. He's the company's legal representative, locally. Came here from the main office. They are nice, solid citizens."

"I liked them. His wife—"

"Rose."

"Yes, Rose. She talked about what church we belonged to. I suppose she does a lot of church work, Needlework Guild, and all that."

"Her church means a great deal to her, yes. You won't have much in common with her, though the judge can be helpful."

"I see."

"Who else? The Hunters, probably."

She searched her memory. "A round, short man who drank beer and had had brain surgery."

"He really did have. A tumor, successfully removed. His wife raises poodles."

"Do the two things go together?"

He smiled.

"There was an unattached woman who actually did use a lorgnette."

"Yes. She needs cataracts removed, and won't acknowledge the fact. She coordinates the schooling of the company children.

"Do they have a school?"

"In Baumgarten? Oh, yes, they do. If you talk too much, you'll find yourself being an aide."

"I'll be careful."

"I devoutly hope so. And, of course, you met Eric Pemscot."

"Big boss."

"He is that. Recently widowed, and the women chase him. He'll appreciate you more if you don't contend."

"You forget—"

"Alster? Not for a minute. And I know your ways of pursuit, too."

Jane laughed aloud. "There was a hearty man who talked about the good hunting. He's promised me a moose."

"Not a *moose,* Jane."

"Well, whatever it is he hunts."

"I can tell you how to escape those gifts. Say you won't accept fish or fowl or animal that has not been cleaned, ready for the pan."

Her eyes widened. "I wouldn't," she agreed.

"All right. Tell Cliff Doty so."

"Then there was this strange couple. Denby?"

"Yes. Lee and Alice. He publishes the company

40

newspaper; she spends her time dyeing her hair and losing weight."

"And speaking of deadly bores, there was this little woman . . ."

The airport runway lights were in sight. "Hilda," Murphy agreed. "Watch her. She knows everything about everything. Just be friendly. She makes a bad enemy."

"Why, Dr. *Anderson!*"

He nodded, and guided the car up a winding ramp.

"Now," said Jane, gathering her purse, checking on her tickets, "now that you've told me about them, what will you tell your friends about me?"

His face in profile, she could see the smile wrinkles deepen about his eyes. Murphy was not a handsome man, but he had a strong, good face, a strong, tall body. His hair was smooth, slightly on the red side. His eyes were deep set, his smile tight. Reserve. That, Jane felt, was Murphy's "quality."

"I'll tell them," he said, preparing to hand the car over to an attendant, "I'll tell them that Alster *is* a good doctor. I'll admit that I know you both well, but I won't talk about you."

"You'll tell them that?"

"Just that I know you well. You will remember that I do."

She remembered.

3

The Friday night dinner group was fun. It could be interesting. Murphy Anderson had enjoyed the companionship of it, the interchange of knowledge and scandal, friendly anecdotes, and occasionally an idea developed and discussed.

This was not a formal club; there was just the "bunch" who ate together at the club, paying their own checks. Sometimes a birthday would occasion a cake baked by one of the women, and some special wine. Occasionally events caused the week's session to be cancelled. But generally the same group appeared, and had a good evening together.

When Murphy resigned as company doctor, he had not attended the Friday night dinners until Eric Pemscot and Kate Beetz made a formal call on him to ask why he had dropped out.

"I moved across the river," said Murphy reasonably.

"Can't you swim?" asked Kate.

"I'll lend you my canoe," said Eric.

Murphy laughed. "OK, you nuts. I'll come. Unless—"

"We know your unlesses," said Kate. "A baby or an appendix or a better offer."

That was it. So, the Friday after Jane Alster had made her appearance, Murphy slipped quietly to a seat on a stool of the club's bar.

"Hiya, Doc," said Cliff Doty. "Where've you been hiding?"

"Where you could reach me by telephone," said Murphy.

"I suppose you think you resigned from us as well as the hospital."

"I often make mistakes."

"Yes, and you cover them up like a cat." Cliff made scrabbling gestures with his hands.

"I haven't made any mistakes, Cliff. Except in my own profession, of course."

They were all glad to see him. Murphy kept his own counsel, but that was allowed a doctor, they declared. In his case. They were not to be so philosophical about Alster. And, of course, before the first forkful of baked shrimp had been eaten that night, someone asked Murphy about Jane, and especially the husband she had represented.

"Didn't you like Jane?" Dr. Anderson asked blandly.

"We liked her, but we don't think we understood her."

"In what way?" asked Murphy, still pretending innocence.

Everybody answered at once, and he put up a hand to silence them. "Look," he said, "you folks are hiring a doctor. And doctors have wives and they have families. Just as you do. But the work Dan Cobb does at the complex is more important than what Helen and her grandchildren do. The work I did was what concerned you."

His friends nodded. "But we still would like to know more about the Alsters," purred Hilda Curren.

"You saw Jane. She was here for three days. Her hair has always been blond, and she had always been pretty and provocative. You can like her, or not, but liking her would be more fun."

"For her."

"For you."

"But we wanted you to stay here, Murphy."

"That was taken out of my hands. Now, as for Alster . . ."

"Does he have a first name?"

"Sure. Richard. Dr. Richard William Alster, a damn fine doctor. But he is also a man who won't give a hoot in the hot place what you think of him."

"What does he look like?"

"Oh, he's dark. Black hair. More of it than I have. Tall. Thin. And a very hard worker."

"His wife mentioned a family."

"Yes," said Murphy, picking up a shrimp, eating it, swallowing it. "He has a family. A son whom you may never meet."

"What . . . ?" asked one of the women.

"Because he's a busy young man, and he is not Jane's son. There was a first marriage. Though, get this, I think Jane and Mike like each other. Then there is a daughter. Margaret. Sixteen or so. As pretty as a field of daisies. She attends a girls' school in Ohio. I think it is Ohio. And of course she is modern about many things. You will like her. I think everyone does."

"They are going to live in the display house," said Alice Denby.

"Well, Jane can cope with it, if anyone can."

"What about the doctor?"

"I am not going to make a single prediction to you about Alster."

"But he's a good doctor," drawled Cliff Doty.

Murphy shot him a glance. "Keep that in mind," he said quietly.

"I think I'll like him," said Helen Cobb. "He sounds so different from his wife."

A couple of the men protested. Jane Alster, they thought, was a clever woman and certainly good looking.

The talk drifted to other things, but Murphy Anderson continued to think about Alster. And Jane. He was feeling troubled, he realized. But Alster could do the work, and he was needed by the complex. They got some pretty complicated surgery because of the logging operations and the sawmills. And any group of three hundred families could stir up enough medical situations to keep a doctor interested and occupied.

Alster had not really jumped at his offer, but he had accepted it, with the perhaps unnecessary explanation that he had been trying to find a location where he could slow down to some degree and spend the rest of his professional life doing some of the things he wanted to do. Meaning his research. Alster had always had some line of research going for him.

Murphy told this, answering some question that Eric Pemscot put to him.

"If he's a scientist . . ."

"Well, he is, of course, but not in the sense you mean, Eric. He has a microscope, and even in that crazy house, certainly in the hospital, he will find a spot, a bench to put his microscope on, and keep notes on whatever he will be doing."

"Here?"

"Why not? We're people here, and that's always what a doctor's research is concerned with."

And eventually the Alsters arrived in person, having driven halfway across the country so that they could keep their car. Some snow beyond Albuquerque had delayed them for a day, but they did arrive.

The people of Baumgarten saw them come, the people at the plant saw them. Hilda Curren announced the arrival of "our new doctor." Then she went on, as was typical of her, to muse about heroes. "Nowadays," she wrote, "the heroes we are familiar with, or used to be, have faded into the shadows of a motley crew named Brown, Lopez, and Miciano. This new man among us has the opportunity and the appearance of a genuine hero, strong jawed, handsome, and proud. The Greeks would have recognized him for what he is."

"What in the blue blazes is she saying?" Louis Hunter asked Kate Beetz.

"That she's fallen for the new doctor."

"Then the man is in trouble. I wonder what the same man will think of her."

No one asked Alster that, but when Murphy called that first evening to inquire as to their welfare, Alster said to him, "It seems we are going to live in one hell of a house, but I am sure I'll be too busy at the hospital to notice."

He was busy. And he liked the hospital. His tall, lean figure fitted the picture people had of top surgeons; he liked Joe Raithel. "The boy's ready to learn and to take orders," he told Jane. She decided that things promised to go well.

"I'm going to give a party," she told her husband. "In the kitchen."

"Why the kitchen?"

"Have you looked at the kitchen?"

"Should I?"

"I think so." She held out her hand and led him.

So he looked at the kitchen, and whistled softly. It was a green kitchen, with a patterned tile floor, the cabinets pale green with white knobs. All the pottery, pans, and dishes were white, banded and nobbed in gold. There were hanging baskets, a topiary tree, and actually a two-foot ceramic statue of a white poodle sitting up to beg. The breakfast room had white furniture, and a view of the mountains and the trees. Alster shrugged.

"I hope I can come to the party."

"Why couldn't you?"

"Well, as of this minute, I have to step over to the hospital. We had an injured man brought in today with crushed ribs and all sorts of things. He has begun to aspirate. So good-bye. When you go to bed, don't fall out and down into the living room."

She laughed. "Good luck with the injured fellow. And I think you are finding our house and your work, both, quite interesting."

He left, without comment.

So the Alsters had arrived. Jane gave her party, which was beautifully done—crème de menthe melon balls in ruby bowls, hot dips and cold, the best Scotch and bourbon—the doctor was charming to each lady in turn.

But, it was said, the company people had better not expect only parties and party charm from the Alsters.

Why? What had happened?

"Oh, nothing really important. Jane Alster couldn't find something she wanted in the Scott stores, and she talks of a chartered bus trip to the shops in San Francisco. And it seems the doctor is setting up rules in the hospital."

"Isn't he supposed to?"

"These must be different. It has something to do with the annual checkups of all adults eligible for medical care. Poor Joe is halfway up the wall."

"Poor Joe" was. He liked Dr. Alster, admired him extravagantly as a surgeon. But the order for his idea of a comprehensive checkup, which he called a "reasonable examination," shocked the young doctor. And he made the mistake of asking Dr. Anderson about it.

"We haven't the time, or the equipment, for what he wants, Doctor."

"Does Alster talk about preventive medicine?"

"Yes, he does, and, of course, I favor that, too. But these examinations . . . And the equipment will cost a terrible sum . . ."

"Tell me about it, Joe," said Murphy. "Though you know, as well as I do, that you should not have appealed to me."

"It's not an appeal, sir. I admire Dr. Alster very much, and I want him to stay. But, besides the work, the time these tests will take . . ."

"And which you will have to conduct."

Joe's face flushed. "Probably most of them," he agreed.

"All right. Dr. Alster won't expect you to be doing other things in the meantime, will he?"

"Well, I wouldn't suppose so. He's putting on another lab technician, one trained in blood chemistry."

"Fine. I'll remember that you have that. Did the office object?"

"I don't suppose so."

"And will you be expected to pay for the expensive equipment?"

Joe laughed. "I'd better not be."

Murphy nodded and settled back into his chair. The two men were sitting on the terrace of Dr. Anderson's small home. On the lawn, Alan, a boy of ten or so, was throwing a Frisbee toward a hedge and evidently hoped to become skilled with the toy.

"Now tell me specifically about these tests," Dr. Anderson said. "Then I'll know if Alster is out of line. He's come to us from the Veterans' setup, you know. Money and time may not be too big a factor for him."

"Yes. Well—he puts signs around, you know, and some of the employees don't like them."

"They have to gripe at something. Stay with the examinations. I suppose there are signs about that?"

"Oh, yes. Reminders that one is required every twelve months." Joe sighed. "And there's a sign in my office and in the labs on what the tests must cover—he's had new test sheets printed, by the way, well, anyway, I could bring you one of the sheets of instructions—the tests must include the usual things, blood count, urinalysis, serology, sedimentation rates, ECG, chemistry profile . . ."

Murphy straightened in his chair, and Joe looked at him. Murphy flipped his hand. "Go on," he said, "if there is more. Lung X-rays, I suppose . . ."

"Oh, yes, sir. Triglyceride count, and a proctosigmoidoscope test."

Murphy whistled. "I see what you mean about time. I suppose the chemistry profile covers all sorts of things—sugar, nitrogen, uric acid, cholesterol, and certain enzymes. All of these things, plus listening to the heart and lungs, checking the blood pressure, and examining the pelvis—"

"And the breasts of the women."

"Yes, of course. This would round out a very effective examination, but I didn't begin to be that thorough. I made a history and a general examination suffice. With Alster's program—who evaluates the results?"

"I do, and he checks on me."

"Doesn't that take a lot of time?"

"You know it does, sir. Of course, in time, I suppose

it will pay off. We'll have a record on every possible patient."

"Some of whom will have gone on to other jobs."

"Yes, sir."

Murphy sat silent. "I think we began by saying you should not tell me these things."

"I know, sir. But the men—and some of the women—they don't like the signs. They didn't want you to leave. And they are rather centering their protest on me."

"On *you?* For Pete's sake, why?"

"They think I am being worked to death."

"And you are?"

"Well, I do keep busy. But I think we can work things out. I admire Dr. Alster, and I hope he will continue with us. His wife is lovely to me, by the way."

"Don't fall in love with her, Joe."

The young doctor laughed. "I don't have time," he said wryly.

Dr. Anderson sat, thoughtful. "Am I supposed to do something?" he asked.

"Oh, no, sir. However, I know you are friends."

"I have known Alster for twenty years. That can mean variety in friendship."

Joe considered the statement. Then he shifted his weight in his chair. "Did you do stomach auscultation, sir? I mean abdominal, of course."

"I did when indicated, Joe."

"I couldn't remember. I was rather upset. Dr. Alster—"

"Did he chew you out?"

"Well, I think so. He—"

"Tell me about it. Since we have already crossed the boundary of propriety."

"Oh, maybe it isn't much. You see, we had this

woman—we still do. Wife of one of the workers. Middle-aged. Late fifties, I think. Sixty perhaps. And she came in with some stomach distress. Pain and general discomfort. I talked to Dr. Alster about her. He asked me, 'What about sounds?' I told him that she complained of rumblings, which embarrassed her. And he asked me if I had auscultated. I didn't understand what he meant."

"He meant, had you used your stethoscope."

"I know he did, and I made the mistake of asking if he meant the stomach. He's very particular about anatomy."

Dr. Anderson laughed.

But Joe sat looking bothered. "He explained that he had meant the use of the stethoscope, and I said no, I had not used it. And he . . ."

"He asked, 'Why not?'" Murphy's voice matched Alster's cold, biting tone.

Joe nodded. "He did just that, sir. And I tried to explain the other tests possible—"

Dr. Anderson was still smiling.

"Oh, of course, he knew about barium tests and all that, but he had me flustered."

"And he knew it."

"Yes, sir. So he gave me a lecture, and a demonstration, on how much could be told by auscultation. How the food progressed; what it meant if there was a silent stretch . . . and *then* he said I could use barium."

"Now I'll ask a question that is certainly out of line."

"Yes, sir?" asked Joe.

"Do you like Dr. Alster? Can you work with him?"

"I admire him as a doctor. Yes, I do, sir. He knows way more than I do, and I can learn from him. But, personally—well, I've never known anyone just like him."

"Don't let that worry you," said Murphy. "Nobody else has ever known an Alster."

Joe decided that he would accept Dr. Anderson's unspoken advice. He would work hard with Dr. Alster, learn as much as he could from him, and above all else he would not discuss the man with anyone. Especially not with Dr. Anderson again. But he did wish—

He watched Alster. He listened to every word he said. The doctor worked hard, and then, without a word to anyone, he would be off the floor. "I think he's in his office, Dr. Raithel," the floor nurse would say. "He asked not to be disturbed."

Sometimes Alster would stay there for fifteen minutes, sometimes for an hour, or more. One could only guess what he did. Sometimes, instead of going into his office, he would go off into the woods. He would be seen striding up the road. Sometimes he would sit down, within sight, and do nothing but lean against a tree and think.

At other times, he would disappear into the green wilderness—to think? What else? He went alone. He might meet someone, but who would that be? The questions refused to answer themselves and some ceased to be asked. But almost everyone agreed that the new doctor was a strange one. A weirdo. Could he do his job, asked Eric Pemscot.

"Oh, yes. He's a very good doctor."

"Then we'll let him be a little weirdo. We all are, in various ways. So we will just wait and see on Alster. By the way, have he and his wife been asked to eat dinner with the rest of us on Friday nights?"

That meant that they must be asked. And sometimes Alster came. Jane almost always did. One evening when she came alone she engaged in a spirited discussion about Alster's looks.

"When he first came here I thought he was handsome," said Agnes Hunter.

"You said he was fabulous," corrected Hilda Curren,

"because he had black onyx cuff links engraved with a caduceus."

Several people laughed. "Are you talking about my husband?" asked Jane from a distance down the table.

"Of course," said Hilda. "We've long ago settled the good looks, or bad, of the other men."

"And you thought Alster was handsome when he first came, and now you are wondering—"

"I think it's his manner that has changed a few points of view," said Judge Lawrence. "He is rather aloof, you know, Jane."

"Does that change his appearance?" she asked with interest, but with no evident rancor.

"It makes us be critical."

"He's as superior as Mount Washington," declared Helen Cobb.

"To everybody?" purred Jane.

Kate Beetz laughed, and so did Hilda. The men were listening with interest.

"What in hell difference do his looks matter?" asked Helen Cobb's husband. "I look like a bald cookie monster, and everyone loves me."

"Yes, we do," Hilda agreed, above the laughter that swept the table.

"Don't you resent his superior manner?" Anne Hother demanded.

"I think he has a right to it. I think he is smarter than the rest of us."

This was not getting them anywhere, so the conversation changed. But the members continued to watch Alster and to discuss him. So did the town, and the church he attended.

As for the employees of the company, there was a growing movement of rejection among them. The men would ask to see Dr. Raithel. The women told stories about Alster. "He's good with children, but he hasn't one bit of use for mothers."

And some of these comments came to Dr. Anderson. "I wish you hadn't left," various ones would say. "This new man . . ."

And Dr. Anderson was troubled. He was responsible for getting Alster to Baumgarten. But his chief concern was for the company, for the men and women who needed a company doctor, preferably a good one. Joe Raithel was not yet ready to carry so heavy a load.

The hospital needed Alster, even more than Alster needed a place where he could work. Dr. Anderson was troubled, to the point where he considered a conference with Jane on the subject. This would be a tricky move. If Alster ever suspected, and Jane's ego was such that she would surely, sooner or later, tell her husband that she and Anderson had kept him on his job . . .

An idea that was just about as bad led Murphy, on a rainy evening, to visit the Alsters. He had been in the display house before, but that evening he walked about as curiously as if he had never seen it before.

"What did you do to it?" he asked Jane.

She shrugged. "Upstairs," she said, "we had to put in shelves and shelves for Alster's books and my Indian artifacts. Down here—cushions."

Murphy nodded. There were cushions indeed. Bright ones, scattered on the curving, green-carpeted steps, which, in addition to the window-seat couches, served as seating accommodations for guests. The bright cushions were all about twenty inches square, soft but resilient. There was a rust-colored one, a patterned one, also rust, a patterned black and white cushion, as well as an all-black one.

Murphy picked up this one and shook his head. "Must it go back where I found it?" he asked.

"Oh, no. But one afternoon, Joe dropped in and said he was tired, he wished he had a cushion to tuck under his shoulders. I fetched one that I had on my bed—it was patchwork and looked awful. But, of course, it rested his spine. The next day, I decided on colors, bought the material, and made the things. They do change the living room, don't they?"

"As much as the lingering aroma of a broiled steak changes your kitchen," Murphy told her.

"Why didn't you come for dinner?" asked Alster.

"I wasn't invited."

"You might have been if you had indicated hunger. Or just have dropped in at five o'clock. That's what Sonny Raithel does. Jane asks him to stay—and he does."

"He talks to me endlessly about his brother," said Jane.

"Do other people know that?" asked Murphy.

"They could."

"And you could, if you'd listen," said Alster dryly. He offered Murphy a brandy glass. "And," he said, turning back to the small bar, "of course Sonny and Jane are rapidly becoming a subject of considerable gossip."

"Alster," said Jane sweetly, "shut up!"

Alster shrugged and went to sit on the couchlike seat before the big window.

"How is Alan?" Jane asked their visitor.

Murphy sniffed the brandy in his glass. "The boy is well," he said. "But he does not progress."

"When we agreed to come here," said Alster coldly, "I was not aware that you would be our chaperone."

"Especially when one is not needed," murmured Jane.

"You came here," said Murphy, ignoring her, "because you wanted and needed a job. I offered you the chance of a good one. I did expect you to recognize that it was—is—good, and try to keep it."

"I have an interesting case over at the hospital," said Alster firmly. For twenty minutes the two doctors talked shop, individual cases, and some background information for Alster, reports on patient progress for Murphy, who knew these people and, in some cases, had previously treated the same ailments that Alster now handled.

When there was a pause in the talk, Jane again asked Murphy, "How's Alan?"—her large blue eyes holding his attention until he answered.

"He's well, thank you," said Murphy.

A little fire flickered on the square hearth and, rising abruptly, Alster added a stick of pungent-smelling wood to it. A flame flared and the room was reflected in the black-glass tiles that surrounded the fire hole.

Murphy was silent for a minute or two, watching the fire. Then he lifted his head. "Alster," he said firmly, "could you and Jane take a little lecture?"

"I couldn't," said Jane quickly. "So excuse me, please? I have some sleeping to do."

Alster glanced at her, and she sat back upon the carpeted step. He turned to Murphy. "Have we got off on the wrong foot?"

Murphy turned his glass in his long, tapered fingers. "It would have been better," he said, "if you had come in here quietly, allowed the people to get to know you, to realize how much you have to give the community. Alster's medical proficiency, as well as the experience gained by his study and his travels. Jane's beauty, her true knack for hospitality—"

"But we . . . ?"

"Yes, you did. You changed rules on the very first day. Your patient check-up orders are extreme, and you know it. Jane gave a charming, but most unusual party for people she did not know and she had not given them an opportunity to know her."

"And . . ." said Alster, his dark eyes sparking.

"My lecture," said Murphy steadily, "would have to do with the drama based upon the rejection of a human being by a sizable, and certainly an important, section of the society in which he is forced to live."

Alster considered what he had said. "You want me to be a country doctor and look to you for advice."

"I do not!" cried Dr. Anderson. "I want to be able to tend to my own practice, without worrying about you in a position you can ably fill, but which you seem to want to turn into a medical example, if not actually an experiment. Good gravy, man! When you get a crunched ankle, treat a crunched ankle! Be friendly, be concerned. But don't issue orders that the employees cannot hunt from deer stands!"

"It's unsportsmanlike."

"It is. He should meet the deer on the ground, on his own level. But that fact, that instruction is not what you are expected to expound upon in the hospital o.r. There you deal with bones and flesh, and reaction, and casts. Do your lecturing, if you absolutely must, at dinner on Friday night, or when meeting some of the company people on the road. Jane . . ."

"Yes!" she said brightly. "What have I done?"

"Can't you make do with a scarf bought here in Baumgarten, or certainly in Scott? Must you organize a safari to take your money and your purchases to San Francisco?"

"I see," said Jane. "I could even, I suppose, subsist on the clothing I already possess."

"I am sure you have enough to serve six women. But for needles and thread, and a scarf of a certain color—"

"Try the local shops."

"And find some charming thing to say about them. They really are not bad. And Scott is not the boondocks."

"Oh, oh," said Alster.

"The point is," said Murphy, "I want to keep you here. The company needs you. It needed me, but circumstances arose over which I had no control."

"You're popular," said Jane.

"That's my native charm. Alster has more of that than I do, but he hoards it as a squirrel hoards nuts."

Alster got to his feet and stood looking out of the window. The tall trees were blowing in a rising wind. "Does it ever snow here?" he asked.

"It certainly does. What do you have on your mind?"

"Eskimos," said Jane, "and now I really am going upstairs to bed. Thanks for coming in, Murphy. Next time come early and get a steak."

She kissed both men and went upstairs. "She's a great girl," said Murphy.

"She can be," Alster agreed. "Now I suppose I had better talk to you about Eskimos."

"Are they pertinent?"

Alster said that they were, and he told about his cholesterol experiments. Would he, should he, could he, continue that work in his present situation?

"Why don't you ask?"

"I am asking."

"I haven't the authority . . ."

"You've certainly acted tonight as if you did have," said Alster.

"That was interested advice I was passing out. I want you to stay here."

After Murphy's call, things went along; perhaps Jane did better. Dr. Alster certainly was busy. Joe Raithel told of his meticulous care of his patients. He set up out-patient hours to suit his convenience; he was a careful and concerned surgeon. And he enjoyed the early approach of spring. Frequently he took his "rest," his free hour or two, to walk up into the woods, where he would sit watching the chipmunks scamper through the yellow pines.

He began to develop his cholesterol experiment again. And vandalism struck the wide-windowed hospital. At dusk rocks would be thrown; one Sunday someone used a tile spade to smash a lower window. And the culprit was immediately identified.

The matter was extensively discussed at the dinner gathering on Friday night.

"That boy of his was the reason we lost Murphy," said Kate Beetz. "I've always resented that."

"You don't think Alster is a substitute?" Jane asked blandly.

"We would never know what we were missing," Kate explained. "If Murphy could have stayed, we wouldn't have known that you and Dr. Alster existed."

"Murphy was not asked to leave," said Eric Pemscot firmly.

"Oh, we know that. But he did leave because of that boy."

"Wouldn't he be better off, himself," asked Helen Cobb, "if the kid were in a school where he could get special education?"

"Alan does get special attention," said Jane, "but he is incorrigible."

"Do you know him?" asked someone down the table.

"We have known Dr. Anderson for fifteen years, at least."

The assembled friends leaned forward with interest. Jane smiled widely. "You won't get an answer to any of your questions," she warned.

"And the boy is not incorrigible," said Alster. "He can learn, he could change—and who of us is without sin? Don't you agree, Miss Oquist?"

"Miss Oquist" was a guest. Eric Pemscot had brought her. A lissome, very pretty brunette. Surprise at her presence had almost covered over the question of the vandalism and the Anderson boy.

"The name is *Oquest*," this new lady now said firmly.

"Oh, no, dear," said Alster. Jane watched him apprehensively. Was he really going off on one of his dissertations? He read everything that came to hand, and he could, at will, talk anything to death.

As he was prepared to do that evening, on the source of names, how they changed, were corrupted—that was the word that offended the boss's date.

"I think," she broke in, "that, Irish or not, my name is the one my father knew and used. And his father before him."

"Would you mind dreadfully?" asked Alster silkily, "if I salved my conscience by calling you Oquist?"

The handsome visitor—she wore a black dress, close fitting, with strings of gold set with ruby-red stones. "I would prefer," she said icily, "that you didn't call me anything at all. A moment ago we were discussing the problems of some boy. I wonder, doctor, if drinking is *your* only problem?"

Alster reached out his fine surgeon's hand to lift the stemmed glass at the side of his plate. It was empty, and had been all through dinner. "I'll answer your query," he said in his biting way of dropping each word like a shard of ice into a bowl of water, "the first time you find me in the operating room under the influence of alcohol." He turned a shoulder toward Miss Oquest, and began a conversation with Kate Beetz. Mr. Pemscot could be heard suggesting to his guest that they leave early . . .

Dr. Anderson heard about the guest, he heard about Alster's attack—or, at least, his skillful knife-cutting on the young woman.

"Who was she?" he asked Hilda Curren. "Why did Eric—?"

"Eric is lonely. Miss Oquest is a saleswoman, and model, for a dress shop in Scott. Really smashing in looks."

"What made her think Alster drinks?"

"He does, at times, Murphy."

"So do we all."

"Aren't doctors different?"

"Not any more than head men of industries. Eric misses his wife. His home has been empty for nearly a year."

"There are more suitable women available."

"Yes, and there are better ways for Alster to release tension than a nip from a bottle kept in his desk's top drawer. That's the gossip, isn't it?"

"Is gossip all that strong? That it could hurt the man?"

"I know of nothing stronger, Hilda, dear. And we want Alster to stay here. We need him. And for his own sake he must stay here."

Hilda studied his face. "You're dead serious, aren't you?"

"Oh, yes, I am. Off the record, I wish my friends would help me to hold him here. He is needed, but the important thing is, he's at the point where failure here could be most destructive. Any man must have pride, a place among his fellow men. Alster occupies that place by his surgical ability. The question is, can we give him the pride he needs to go with it?"

"You can try . . ." said Hilda softly.

"I must try," said Murphy Anderson. "I must try."

4

Dr. Alster might have come in as company doctor and scarcely been noticed. But because he was the kind of man he was, because he lived in the display house, where no one else had cared to live previously, because he had an attractive and often aggressive wife, there was much talk about the new doctor. And, as happens nearly always, the people who talked—in this case those who lived in the pleasant little town of Baumgarten—soon became polarized. There were those who could find nothing good to say about the Alsters and just as many, perhaps a few more, who acknowledged that they were "different" but, on the whole, a good thing to have happen to the locality.

"We were getting dreadfully stodgy," Hilda Curren told people. Kate Beetz also took up their championship. She wanted a fisherman-knit sweater to send to a nephew, like the one Dr. A. wore. "He has such good taste in clothes."

Both she and Hilda argued with anyone who would listen. Accept the Alsters, watch them, learn from them, they said. They can bring change into your lives—and fun.

And they proceeded to demonstrate those truths. But

they did not stop the talk, pro and con. Oh, if someone became ill, or was injured, Dr. Alster was admittedly a fine person to have around. But why didn't he join a church? He attended, but he didn't belong.

Why didn't Jane work for the blood bank, or help deliver meals to the old and sick?

It was said that she did spend one day a week at the day-care center, and that the children adored her. Being a nurse (or so she claimed—she claimed so many things) she could be useful in many ways. She *was* useful. She taught crafts to the old people at the low-cost housing center in Scott—but she had a difficult time finding a shop to cut and shampoo her hair. . . .

So things went. Alster was aware of the polarization; Jane said he was imagining things. Was he going through with the music plan?

"Hilda Curren says I should."

"Hilda."

"She's public relations, and I rather like the funny little bitch."

"She rather likes you. So does Kate Beetz."

"Haven't they been nice to you?"

"I don't know. I hardly give them the chance. When is the concert?"

"Tuesday, at noon."

On Tuesday, at noon, the members of the small but excellent symphony orchestra of Scott—some of them amateurs—gave a concert beside the pond on the central mall of the complex. They played for an hour to catch two shifts of workers, some of whom brought their sandwiches and coffee out of doors. Dr. Alster did, sitting on the coping of the walk that separated the hospital from the main roadway. Windows were opened.

"On the whole," Hilda told Mr. Pemscot, "I think it

was a success. Can we try the piped-in music every day?"

"The men don't like Muzak."

"This won't be Muzak."

"Who selects the music?"

"We're using Dr. Alster's library of tapes, but suggestions will be welcome."

"At noon?"

"At any time. Oh, you mean the music. Yes, at noontime."

"Is Alster paying for this?"

"The symphony volunteered. Hoping to get subscribers, of course. Alster asked a professional to install the speakers."

"Would he let the company pay?"

"I expect so. Ask him."

Pemscot had been cool to Alster since the Oquest-Oquist matter, but he was businessman enough to know that an hour's relaxation would benefit his factory workers. The whole matter was settled, at Alster's request, so that only a few people knew that he was the man behind the noontime concerts.

But still, a proportion of workers said the music spoiled their handball games, that they liked to read the morning paper . . .

Dr. Anderson asked about the percentage of dissenters. Dr. Alster shrugged. "We'll do it during the warm weather months. That gives rights to the ones who don't like music."

"Handball in a cold wind is something else again," said Anderson wryly.

"It also can be played to music."

And there the matter rested.

Score one for Alster, Hilda told Murphy.

"I hope you are right," said that doctor. But he believed that she was, to the point that he said so to Alster. Who shrugged again.

"Look here, man!" said Murphy angrily. "You need friends."

Alster nodded. "I understand that everyone does. You, too?"

"Certainly me too."

"Did you know?" asked Alster, rubbing his stethoscope against the sleeve of his white jacket, "that it is claimed that it was the abandonment of fraternities in the sixties that spawned violence and revolutionary activities on the campuses? Now the frats are back and we have quiet."

Murphy looked at his friend and said, with exasperation, that Alster was the most skillful subject changer he had ever known.

"I didn't change the subject, Doctor. I was agreeing with you that I must devote some time to acquiring a few friends and loyal cohorts."

"Do you know what caused what developments on the campuses? Who broke up the frats? And who put them together again?"

Alster laughed. "You see through a thing so clearly, Doc."

"Yes, I do. So watch it, will you? Try to get along here, will you?"

"I am trying."

"Even if you get bored. And keep a thumb on our girl Jane, too, will you?"

"Look, man. I came here to do medicine. I came here to do a good job of it, too. If I would be allowed."

"I think you can be allowed, Alster. Just take things a little more slowly here at first. People will learn your ways, find out that you know your medicine, and they will accept you."

"Some men can work at my type of job and not need to have a single friend of the sort you mean."

"Hermits, yes. But you don't happen to be one."

Alster smiled. "No," he agreed. "At least I never have been."

Dr. Anderson sat thoughtful. "I didn't bring you out here to be your mentor and adviser, you know."

"I wouldn't have come under such conditions. I have always been my own man, Murph."

"Yes, I know that. But, before this, your own ideas have caused trouble. This time, this trouble, such as it is—and as I don't want to see grow—has been on the personal side. You've always got along with *people*, Alster. You know how. I've heard you called charming."

"Well, I am, of course," said Alster sourly.

"At least you know how to be. You seem to make Jane happy."

Alster's head snapped up, and his black eyes stared at Dr. Anderson.

"All right, all right," Murphy conceded. "But if not your wife, you make some woman happy. Your girl of the minute must be satisfied with your efforts."

"What girl?" asked Alster.

Murphy laughed, and prepared to leave. "I am interested only in the effort you have always seemed able to make."

"I prefer to attend to my doctoring," said Alster as the door closed on his friend. At least, Dr. Anderson had come in the spirit of friendship.

Dr. Alster agreed within himself to try to "get along." He went to the Friday-night dinners. He continued to supply the noontime concerts. He talked to the patients who came to him, showing interest in their homes, their families, their backgrounds. But he had always done that. And he was a capable doctor. He had always been *that*.

Alster himself never did know just what started the fire. He had been ready to accept Murphy's advice, obliquely given, and settle down to medicine as it was taught and practiced. Of course he would, and did, continue his cholesterol research. But he spoke of that to Pemscot, and Pemscot agreed that it would be an interesting, and harmless, thing to do. Then he had mentioned the pool. Was that it?

That *was* it! It had to be the flint rubbed into flame. The Alsters had been told, when they first came to the complex, that the doctor could have a pool. One was in the original plan for the display house. There were sketches, pictures, and the company was ready to build it if Dr. Alster . . .

Dr. Alster definitely was interested. So interested that it was told he had helped dig the hole, which he had not, though he was on the site often and did get his hand into the construction; and he personally planted the begonias in the curve of the pretty free-form pool; he could be seen tamping down the sod, which completed the landscaping.

The pool was small, but a man could have a plunge early in the morning, and at midnight. And Jane, wearing a bathing suit, a shift, or nothing at all, it was said, could sunbathe. Maybe the stories were true, maybe not. She could have worn an Annette Kellerman, and a filthy-minded person still could have made up the stories. A filthy mind—perhaps some youngster heard his elders talking—something of that sort could have begun the thing . . .

Jane told Alster that Rose Oquest had telephoned to tell her that Jane's name and telephone number had been scrawled on the wall of the men's room of the company cafeteria, and that she was described as being "Available."

"How does the Oquist woman know such a thing?" Alster asked, not looking up from some notes he was making at the small table that served them for meals. So far, Jane had not resumed her "writing."

At first, he did not really listen to what Jane said in answer, but he caught enough of the gist of what she said in reply to make him lay his pen down and look up at her.

"You're going to do *what?*" he asked.

"I am going to the cafeteria manager, and if I don't get action, I'll go to Eric Pemscot himself. They are going to get that loathsome graffiti off the wall, or I will sue in court."

Alster sighed and picked up his pen. "You will do no such thing," he said softly.

"But—"

"I could speak of biting the hand that feeds you, and find other clichés. Instead—"

"Will you go see for yourself?"

"I will not. I don't use the men's room at the cafeteria. And I would not believe that Oquist woman if she told me the color shirt I am wearing."

"Alster . . ."

"*Jane!* Just forget the whole thing."

"And stop sunbathing?"

"Not if you enjoy it."

Jane herself must have done some talking because the cafeteria manager sought out Dr. Alster and protested that he could not be blamed for what someone else had written on the men's-room wall.

"You clean those walls regularly, I presume," said Dr. Alster.

"The company's cleaning crew attends to that, sir."

"All right, Bommarito. And I am sure no harm has been done."

"Well, I sure hope so, sir. Mrs. Alster seems to be a very nice lady."

"I think you are right. She does seem to be."

Alster was angry. He did not like anyone's finger touching his name. But he was sure Murphy would have advised his action.

Murphy was present at the second incident. It was said that he had been the one to organize, or consolidate, the group that ate dinner together every Friday night. The country club was not a company project, but the majority of the group's members were connected, in one capacity or the other, with the company. This "club" was a loosely organized affair comprised of congenial souls choosing to eat together. The Alsters quickly had been made members, and even the doctor seemed to enjoy the company.

The women semidressed. They wore long dresses, usually, or pretty pants suits, though not their most formal costumes of that nature. The drinks were individually ordered and went on each member's bar bill. The meal could be ordered from the menu, but the evening's specialty was generally eaten, and enjoyed. Sometimes a member would bring in a special dish—a birthday cake, some novelty salad or casserole lately experienced and enjoyed, but always with the chef's knowledge and agreement. Jane once had made tortoni to loud cheers of approval.

So the Alsters had become a definite part of the "club," liking or not caring for the other members, as happens in any group. On this particular evening, the full roster of fourteen was present. Eric Pemscot had not invited Rose Oquest. But Murphy Anderson had come over from Scott and was solemmly assured that he fully took the place of Pemscot's Rose. There was some rather bawdy teasing on the subject.

"Judge" Lawrence and his wife, Marian, were the last to arrive. Marian slipped into a chair beside Murphy, while the Judge took the chair at the head of the table. Only because it was empty; no one ever wanted to sit there. The meal was being served and he asked the bar attendant to bring a bottle of wine—a certain Burgundy. "And enough glasses for those who appreciate it," he said.

Judge was well liked, and certainly respected. The wine served, and the good onion soup ready to be eaten, he took a folded piece of paper from his vest pocket, and handed it down the table to Dr. Alster. "I thought that this did not need to be displayed," he said.

Alster read what the paper contained, his lips tightening, his eyes hardening. "Where did you get this?" he asked.

"It was on the club bulletin board. I always look to be sure I am not in trouble with my fees and dues. Not much of a poet, whoever wrote it."

Kate Beetz offered to take the paper from Alster's hand.

He stuck it in his jacket pocket. "I think the judge is right," he said. "It should not be read."

"I read it," said Helen Cobb. "I thought it was funny."

"You make a strange friend," Alster told her.

Helen shrugged. "I'd be flattered if someone wrote poetry about me."

"What poetry did they write about whom?" asked Hilda Curren.

"It was not poetry. Not even good doggerel," said

Alster. "Eat your soup and shut up."

"Look, Doctor, I am not your wife, nor your hired office nurse—so don't tell me to shut up."

"I'm sorry," said Alster, "but, please, do eat your soup."

"Was your poem about me?" Jane's clear voice asked from down the table.

"Let it alone, Jane," Murphy advised her.

She got up from her chair and came toward Alster. She was wearing an amethyst-colored blouse with a pair of well-cut grey slacks, silk, and pretty. Her hair was burnished into a pale-gold cap.

She held her hand out to Alster. A long, slender hand, perfectly manicured. She was a beautiful woman.

"If that's another graffiti," she said.

Her husband looked at the others around the table. "Shame to let this soup go cold," he mused. Then his tone brightened. "How many of you saw this thing on the bulletin board?"

Four or five hands went up. "Let her read it," said Hilda Curren. "Someone is going to quote it to her. I saw morning golfers reading it. You don't have a top secret document in your camel's-hair pocket, Doctor."

"No, I suppose not." He took out the square of paper, handed it across his shoulder to Jane, and began to eat his soup.

She stood where she was, reading the five or six lines. Some of her friends laughed, others professed to be interested in the food set before them.

Jane's lips moved, and she read it half-aloud. "Whoever wrote it needs lessons," she said. Then she raised her voice, and read again.

> *I never saw a nudey Jane*
> *But I still hope to see one.*
> *If the sun stays out,*
> *And Joe steps aside,*
> *Maybe the rest of us guys*
> *Will have some fun.*

She threw the paper down and went back to her chair. "How did that thing get on the board?" she asked stiffly.

"A thumbtack will do it, dear," said one of the men.

She flashed him a look of clarified fury.

"How long has it been there?" asked Dr. Anderson. "That's the important question."

He was angry. Perhaps not angrier than Jane or Alster. "The important thing is," he said tightly, "that I was instrumental in bringing in a good doctor to the plant hospital. Do you people want to keep him or not?"

Mr. Pemscot rose to his feet. "You are right, Murphy," he agreed. And he went out of the alcovelike room where their table was set, coming back with the club manager. He told that gentleman what had happened.

The manager was inclined to protest. He said he had no control over what was posted on the board.

"You have control over how long a thing like that stays there. I assume you knew it was drawing attention."

"Well, sir—"

"I'll turn the matter over to Judge Lawrence. He's a lawyer and can tell you what rights Mrs. Alster has."

"It doesn't mention her by name."

"When you read it, did you think it was Mrs. Alster?" asked the lawyer.

"Well, yes, sir. And 'Joe' would be the young doctor.

I've seen them together. But, Mr. Lawrence, I can't always stop and read what folks put on the bulletin board."

"Could your secretary or someone do that for you?"

"Well, I suppose they could."

"Didn't you realize that this particular item was attracting unusual notice?"

"Well, I guess so."

"And you read it?"

"Yes, I did, sir." The man knew that he was in trouble.

"But you didn't take it down."

"No, sir. The members leave notes for each other, and all sorts of things. I'd get hell if I—"

"You stand to get hell for not removing this scurrilous bulletin."

"I beg pardon, sir?"

"I'm sorry," said the dignified attorney. "Scurrilous means scandalous—or dirty, if you prefer."

The manager turned to Jane, then looked at Alster. "I am sorry it happened, sir," he said. "But I couldn't take down a notice some member had posted."

"That is exactly where you got yourself into trouble, my friend," said Alster. "You had the power and the right to remove the damn thing, but you elected deliberately to leave it there."

"He's right," agreed the judge. "And he can sue you personally on that ground."

"But, Judge . . ." said the poor man. "If the club committee, even now . . ."

"That's right," said Mr. Pemscot. "Even now the committee could and should take some action."

"But if they do not," said Judge Lawrence, "I would say that any suit the Alsters, or even Dr. Raithel, would care to file would merit payment out of court.

Because such a case would win in court."

"Yes, sir," said the flustered manager, and at a nod from the judge, he departed.

There was an instant rising flurry of talk. How much would Jane get? How much could she get? Cliff Doty said he could write a better poem with a bad ballpoint.

"I wouldn't try it if I were you," Jane told him. "I'll sue the club, or maybe I'll just go home and sew some ruffles on my bikinis. Especially the green and white polka-dotted one." Her grin was pert. "Which would be better, Alster?" she called to him. "Or worse?"

"Eat your dinner," said her husband grimly.

"I think you should sue," said Murphy.

"I don't agree," Alster told him.

"You never do," said Murphy.

"Well, I'll agree on that," Alster assured him. Someone laughed, and the others joined in.

"Do you think he'll beat Jane when they get home?" Helen Cobb asked of no one in particular.

"Why don't you go round to the back of their house and see?" suggested Hilda Curren.

Murphy stood up. "See here!" he said firmly. "I think we should find something else to talk about."

"I have a very interesting case of ischemic heart disease," said Alster, leaning back in his chair.

"That will do nicely," said Murphy. "We can use up a whole evening explaining to our so-called friends what you mean."

And a couple of the members laughed. "I only hope I never get it," declared Cliff Doty. "Sounds awful."

The country club apologized to the Alsters. That was known. But whether any money was exchanged was doubtful. Dr. Alster refused to talk about the matter, and those who tried to get a reaction from Jane were met by her hand clapped over her mouth and a firm shake of her head.

It was decided that there would be no suit.

"And no more poetry, we hope," said Hilda Curren. "Though anyone of our bunch could write a better verse."

"Wouldn't that make a fun party?" asked Helen Cobb.

"Save it for the Fourth of July," said Hilda. "And then Alster is apt as not to drop his punk stick into the skyrocket box. That night at the club he was not amused."

Nor was he in the days that followed. Even in the hospital, which he ruled sternly, patches of scandal began to crop up like fungus, and that was not a good situation. He discussed the matter with Mr. Pemscot, who asked him if he had talked to Joe Raithel.

"About what?" asked Alster.

"His name is being coupled with Jane's."

"She has always been kind to my interns and residents. Usually they like it."

"I think Raithel may like it. But it isn't good talk we have here, Dr. Alster."

"No, I suppose it isn't. Though, if they were guilty, they would be more discreet. I've seen a lot of things bud, blossom, and fade. I've a little youthful knowledge of my own. But if Jane passes the man on the street and gives him a friendly 'Hi!'—she's friendly to everyone, Pemscot."

"I know she is. Does she—er—have a family she could visit?"

"You mean a logical get-her-out-of-town?"

"It might help. Let things quiet down."

"Yes, it might. Oh, of course, we have a daughter in school. My son is fond of Jane. Perhaps one of her projects—Indian art, or the writing she does . . ."

"Mmmm. Would she agree?"

"If she doesn't, I'll find a seminar for Joe. Though honestly I don't think there is anything but friendly interest there."

"You're probably right. Unfortunately, Joe has a mother who thinks every unattached female is after her son."

"Oh, dear. Though Jane is not unattached."

"She does pretty well what she pleases, doesn't she?"

"Within limits, yes, she does. I'll see what I can think up."

What he thought up was a trip to Taos. At first, he was going too; he even told Jane what clothes to pack for him. But at the last minute the ischemic heart case developed a real block and he had to take the man to San Francisco. Jane went to Taos alone and enjoyed her week there. She even brought back sketches—and a broomstick skirt that swirled prettily about her bare ankles and feet. "Better than ruffles on the bikinis," Kate Beetz told her.

"What went on while I was away?" asked Jane.

"Well—that's hard to say."

"I know Alster took a patient to San Francisco."

"He did, and came right back because Joe's brother took a turn for the worse. Where does he live? Sacramento? Anyway, Joe's crazy about him."

"The man has leukemia."

"That's bad, isn't it?"

"Very bad. Did the town believe his brother was ill?"

"Not the whole town. People kept calling his mother and asking where he was."

"Oh, dear. And she—"

"Yes. She found out about the sweet and hot talk there was about you and Joe."

"The fat got in the fire then, I am sure."

"It did. She said she was going to make him give up his job at the hospital."

"Poor Joe. It might be better if there were some truth in what she heard."

"You can find that out for yourself," said Kate.

Jane looked at her. "What are you suggesting?"

"We'll drive downtown and you can see for yourself."

"I don't want to. Graffiti again?"

"Graffiti. On the apartment building where everyone stops for that long light change at the highway."

Jane said something beneath her breath. "It's a very big apartment house," she said aloud.

"Big enough for spray paint."

"What . . . ?" Jane looked both angry and frightened.

"Oh—*Jane*—and *Joe,* and then *Go, go, go!*"

Jane sat, thoughtful and distressed. "There are a lot of Janes," she said.

"Not in Baumgarten."

"Is it still there?"

"Traces of it. The police moved in when Alster filed suit."

"He . . . ?" Jane's eyes widened. "He didn't!" she declared.

"Oh, yes, he did. And offered an award for the artist in question."

"He has not said one word to me."

"Have you seen much of *him*?"

"Well, not really. I came in last night. He left before I got up this morning. Hmmm. Graffiti. And he finally did sue."

"Judge says he can't win a judgment on this."

"Why not?"

"The dirty words were not on private premises but on a building in plain sight of passing pedestrians. Judge says that makes the difference, the owner cannot be blamed for libel, which is what Alster called it. He said the owner had no control over who read it, and that his role in making it public was too minor to justify legal liability."

"He said all that?"

"He did. To Alster."

"Who chose the one case where he didn't have a case. Gee whiz, Kate . . ." She got up and paced the grass around the pool. "I am so *angry!*" she said.

"You've something else to be angry about," Kate warned her.

Jane whirled, the skirt ballooning out in the sunlight. "What . . . ?"

"Joe Raithel. He's a good doctor, Alster says. But the ninny actually said he did not see how his mother could be upset, or anyone believe there was anything going on between you two—He meant the separate trips not really being separate, him to Sacramento, you to Taos. He said that he could prove he went to see his brother, and besides you were too old for him to want to risk an affair with you."

"And people are laughing about that," said Jane furiously. "Did Alster laugh?"

"I don't see much of him, Jane."

"I'll bet he's mad because the case he chose to file suit on was the one that he couldn't win. Alster hates to be wrong."

"Look . . ." said Kate, then stopped.

"What is it?"

"Oh, nothing maybe. But if I were you, which I am not, I would spend quite a long time with the very attractive husband you have, and tell Joe

Raithel to go peddle his papers."

"There's nothing *there,* Kate!"

"We are talking about what people think is there. But—as I say—" She prepared to leave. "Good luck," she called over her shoulder.

Jane was angry, and as the day went on, she became ever more angry. She worked furiously in the house. Because of abundant, well-paid employment by the company, household help was practically nonexistent. Her home was not hard to keep clean. Alster was a tidy man. That day she sent clothes to the cleaner, she did a washing and drying in the machines in her own house. She changed beds and wiped windows . . .

And when Alster finally did show up, looking tired, she told him that she was planning a barbecue supper instead of the Friday-night dinner at the club.

He turned to look at her. "With an idea in mind?" he asked.

"Yes, I do have. Murphy has told us to make friends."

"We already know these people; they know us. Some want to be friends, some don't."

"But they would all come to a barbecue."

"No doubt. To see what the Alsters are up to now."

"We never have been up to anything."

"I think we must have been. No, Jane. No barbecue at this time. You have an idea, but it's a wrong one. You'd never still the gossip by more talk. I think you should find something to interest yourself in, nothing concerned with the hospital—"

"And Joe Raithel." Her eyes held his.

"And my assistant, yes. He is a good doctor. I am training him to be a better one. He has been able to make people laugh at you without knowing that he did so. Let things lie there. Can't you get up a class in needlepoint, or give more time at the old-folks center

82

in Scott—or maybe write that book you've begun so often and never finished?"

"You mean that, don't you?"

"Yes, I do. I filed suit in your behalf and felt required to withdraw it. Now suppose we make the Alsters the invisible family for a while."

"I've done nothing."

"But be beautiful and friendly. It seems that is too much."

"Before this you've been the one to—"

"I know it, and look where it got me."

She smiled. She would try Kate's advice. "Married to me," she said softly.

"Are you sorry?"

"Not up to now."

"Can't you and I barbecue? Remember, I bought a stove."

"Good! And anyone hungry who smells the steaks can be told we prefer to be alone. Then, afterward . . ."

"That, too, and later," he promised, laughing. "But after the steaks, and we have enjoyed the sunset, I am planning to get out my records on the cholesterol project."

"It got you into trouble—"

"In a government hospital, yes. But Pemscot's okayed it here. And you can help keep my records."

"Will you get subjects?"

"I plan to talk to a meeting of volunteers tomorrow."

"Explain the whole thing?"

"Yes, the women and the men. It should work."

"Yes, it should. Do you want to start the fire?"

"It's a cool evening."

"Put on your plaid jacket. We can eat inside."

The barbecue was delicious, and its odors did draw willing guests, but they were given a drink and asked to withdraw. Jane had been out of town—Alster hoped for a free evening with his wife—

"I hope the word gets spread around about that!" said the doctor, enjoying the stuffed tomato she had cooked in heavy foil. The steaks were supreme.

The meeting on the cholesterol project went well, too. Alster divided the group of those willing to cooperate. "I have no-fat menu meals here for a month," he told those on the diet. "I do hope you will follow them closely, and just think about the chocolate eclairs and deviled eggs you can have next month."

Thirty-five volunteers showed up and that encouraged Alster. Jane set about keeping the books. "Mr. Pemscot asked if he could join," she told Alster.

"Refer all questions to me."

"But—" Then she nodded. "Yes, Doctor," she said mildly.

"It shouldn't be a secret, but I've not told anyone that you are my bookkeeper."

"Maybe they will raise your pay if they think you are doing it all."

Mr. Pemscot did join the project, but Alster still ran into a problem with the office-records department.

Every employee—man, woman, and boy—had to have a physical examination on employment, and was required to have a physical checkup every six months. These records were kept in the hospital files and as such were top secret.

Except to the doctor in charge. Or so Alster assumed. Until one of the men, head of the veneer department, came to him and asked to be given his physical records.

"Why?" asked Dr. Alster, who was tired after a morning of surgery. "Are you leaving the plant?" It was a natural question, he thought.

The man he talked to was a big fellow with bristly

white-blond hair and weathered red cheeks.

"No, I'm not leaving the plant," said this fellow. "I'm a boss and I have seniority."

"Then why—?"

"I just want my private records private to me."

"And to the doctor," said Alster quietly. If possible, he was not going to get into a fight with this chap, whose name was Thompson.

"You work in the veneer department, you say."

"I'm foreman."

"That's a specialized job, Thompson."

"It sure as hell is. And—"

"Do you let many people come in and tell you how to run that job?"

"I sure don't."

Alster sat silent, his dark eyes on the man's face.

"You're doing some sort of experiment . . ." said Thompson uneasily.

"A test of the effect of diet on the heart and arteries, yes," said the doctor. "Have some of your men volunteered for it?"

"I don't know. But I do know I want to protect the guys under me."

"Would you like to arrange a meeting where I could explain the project to them?"

"I want their records under my control."

"I can't give them to you, Thompson. That would be going against the rules of my job."

"Who says?"

"The ethics of my profession."

"Isn't there some way the records of my men could be put in a separate, safe place, where you can't add stuff to them?"

"I don't know what you mean by stuff. I was hired as an expert in medical matters. You were hired to cut and dress veneer wood. We are both trusted to do our jobs, and should trust each other. If you want to forbid your men joining the cholesterol experiment, I suppose Mr. Pemscot would allow it. If asked. He is in it, by the way."

Thompson heaved himself out of the chair. "There's no way I can win, is there?" he demanded sulkily.

Dr. Alster stood up. He still wore his surgical gown, and he looked tired. "I don't see anyplace where you can lose in this, Thompson," he said, seeing the man to the door.

He changed his clothes, looked at his postoperatives, and told Dr. Raithel he was checking out for an hour. Maybe two.

"Yes, sir," said Joe. "When you come back, could I talk to you?"

"Why not?" asked Alster, going down the corridor.

Outside he met Hilda Curren, and she asked him why he had such a "concentrated" frown.

Alster laughed. "I've a busy morning behind me," he told her. "Now I am taking an hour's walk to get over it."

"Can I come along?"

"Sure. And we'll get graffiti somewhere about us."

"Where are we going?"

"Up the hill."

"Could we do otherwise?"

"We could go downhill."

"Yes, we could." She struck out beside him, trotting now and then to keep up with his longer stride. She wore a red sweater and red skirt and, as always, a little hat on her head. He told her about Thompson's visit. "He wants his men's records put into escrow. Why can't people understand as simple an experiment as my cholesterol project?"

"Could I put something in the paper about it?"

86

"About the project, yes. About Thompson, no. I'm afraid I may have clamped down on the wrong man there."

"Tell me about the project."

So he told her about his efforts and results at the veterans' hospital, his interest in what his results would be here. And they walked up and up the logging road. He talked about cholesterol. "We have to have some in our bodies," he said. "And the accumulation of too much of it in our arteries may not be due to what we eat. Or not to that alone." He stopped still in the middle of the dusty road.

"What now?" asked Hilda.

"I know why Thompson came to see me," he said.

"Why? Can I sit down for a minute?"

"Sure. There's always a stump in a lumber-company woods. He came, Hilda, to tell me that I can't use company files for my own purposes."

"I see. And the difference lies in the interpretation of those purposes."

"That's right. Can you make another half mile? I want to show you something."

She groaned and stood up. "How many half miles have we gone? All uphill."

He took her arm, and soon they stopped. "Look," said Alster, pointing downward.

She looked at the pleasant valley below them. The face of the mountain rising on the far side formed a background of rich green pines, spruce and fir trees; a swift little stream bubbled and raced downhill, beside it stood a house, a square box of a house, its wooden plank sides and its roof weathered brown. There were a few aspen trees—the little valley was a peaceful place.

"I come here often," said Alster, sitting down on the rocky ground. Hilda followed suit.

"A prospector's shack," she said.

"I want to buy it," said Alster.

She turned to look at him in disbelief. "You don't want it. Besides, you couldn't. It's on company land. Oh, I suppose they would let you and Jane . . ."

Alster chuckled. "It's empty except for an old rusty stove and a fine collection of cobwebs. Two rooms up, two down. But just to look down at it brings peace to my soul."

She touched his hand. "You're a strange man, Dr. Alster."

"And you are a slow learner," he assured her.

"Has Jane seen this?"

"Of course not. She would burn the thing down before she would live in it."

"But you—"

"Yes, I could live in it. A fireplace, bunk beds, bookshelves, the sound of that mini-river at night—" He glanced at his wrist.

"Now!" he said. "We have to run all the way downhill to the hospital."

"And I can't print a picture of your dream castle?"

"Don't you dare! So, come along. I think Joe Raithel plans to resign."

She turned in alarm. "Oh, no!"

"Oh, no, I shan't let him. But I do have to let him offer."

They ran, they stumbled, they laughed, and even Alster was breathless when they came to the hospital. Hilda said she had other places to go—

Alster went in, stamping the dust from his shoes, brushing dust and debris of dried leaves and needles from his brown plaid trousers.

He went to his office, changed to whites, and buzzed to ask Dr. Raithel to come in, if he wanted to and was not busy. "And send me a glass of milk and some sort of sandwich, please. I wasted my noon hour."

Joe Raithel himself brought in the tray. He had met the orderly in the hall, he said, "and we may not have overmuch time to talk. Maternity alerted me twenty minutes ago."

Alster nodded. "You've seen the mother?"

"Oh, yes, sir. And they'll beep."

"All right, then, let's get on with the milk and the roast-beef sandwich—and whatever it is you want to talk about."

"Yes, sir." Joe sat down. He was a good-looking young fellow with smooth, light-brown hair, parted and swept across his brow. His face was well featured, with high color in his cheeks. Today he wore a red necktie with a white shirt under his white jacket.

"I want," he said, "no, I think I *must* offer you my resignation, sir."

Alster took a deep drink of milk. "Reason?" he asked.

"There's been a lot of misunderstanding, Doctor, about Mrs. Alster's friendliness to me."

Alster nodded. "Jane's a friendly person."

"Yes, she is, sir. And there is no reason—"

"There is no reason for you to resign. Besides, you can't do it, Raithel."

"But—"

"What would you do? As a doctor?"

"Well, I don't really know. Go into private practice, perhaps."

"Yes, you could do that," Alster agreed. "But you have forgotten that I need you here."

"Yes, sir . . ."

"And you need what I can help you learn here."

"I know that, sir. But— Oh, *blazes!*" His beeper was sounding.

"That's it," said the doctor. "So get to work. I'll do the same."

89

Dr. Raithel stood up. "I— Thank you, sir."
Dr. Alster nodded. "Get going, will you?"

The day turned out to be warm, and that evening a half dozen of their friends came to the Alster home, ready and willing to use the pool. It was a pretty thing, located against a hedge of dark trees. A wide sand apron around it offered lounge chairs and big cushions; a flight of steps led to the back porch of the house. Jane made a valiant effort to keep blooming flowers in the right places.

Tonight their friends swam, then gathered around the doctor where he lay stretched out as flat as possible on a chaise.

"You asleep, Doc?" asked Agnes Hunter.

"He's tired," said Hilda Curren. "He took a ten-mile walk at his noon hour today."

Alster opened one eye warningly.

"I didn't say where," she hurried to say, "and I don't think you'll get docked for loafing on your noon hour."

Alster sat up straight, and reached for his shirt; once the sun was gone, the evening would cool. "If a man," he said, "walks in the woods for love of them, half—in this case, part—of each day, he is in danger of being regarded as a loafer. But if he spends that day as a speculator, shearing off those woods and making the earth bald before its time, he is esteemed as an industrious and enterprising citizen. As if there were no interest in forests but to cut them down."

"You're an ecologist, aren't you?" asked Agnes Hunter.

"To a degree," said Alster. "I admit the necessity for the lumbering business, since it gives me a job, a home—"

"And a swimming pool," added Jane.

"And a swimming pool," her husband agreed. "But I refuse to consider the walk I took at noon as loafing."

"I wouldn't suggest any such thing," said Hilda, rubbing her foot.

"You didn't walk with him!" protested someone.

"I learn the hard way," she retorted. "But it was interesting. Tell me, Alster—"

"I don't know why everyone calls me Alster," he answered quickly.

"It comes easy. And Jane calls you that."

"For heaven's sake . . ." said her husband in alarm.

"I wouldn't even try to follow her example," said Hilda hurriedly.

"You couldn't," said Helen Cobb silkily.

"Thank you, darling. And will you please let me finish my question for Alster?"

There was a silence.

Hilda looked around the group. "I guess I'll go on and ask my question," she said. "I wanted to know about this cholesterol project our doctor is working on. Or conducting—whatever the word is. I understand some of the men are afraid of it."

Alster sighed. "I could tell them of the results I've had previously. In the first place, only volunteers are going along with it. This time I have both women and men, and that is interesting. You're on it, Hilda. You know it's a matter of what you eat, or don't eat."

"If you've done it before, why . . . ?" asked Agnes Hunter.

"Why do I do it again?" asked the doctor. "Because situations are different in different locations. The last time I tried my experiments, I was in the Middle West."

"They eat more meat and potatoes," Jane offered.

"Out here, you run to fish and fruits. Not exclusively, but as a major diet."

"I see," said Hilda. "You are trying to connect cholesterol buildup to diet."

"Or not," said Alster. He again mentioned the Japanese and the Eskimos.

"And what will you do with the results?" asked Hunter.

"Offer them in the form of a paper to the medical association."

"Will Jane write it up for you?"

"Not this time; though, before this, she has kept my records."

"She says she is a writer."

"She is," said Alster dryly, "when she writes."

Jane made a sound that was not a laugh, nor was it a profane word or two.

"What have you written?" Hilda asked her firmly.

"I free lance. It depends on when and where Alster is working," said Jane. "If there is a protest here, I could do a sort of satirical thing about labor protests. Over something as harmless as these cholesterol tests."

"He wouldn't let me mention the protests in an article for my paper," said Hilda.

"You aren't married to him, dear," cooed Jane.

Hilda glanced at Alster. "Shall we say it together?" she asked.

He laughed. "I don't care. As you brought out, you are not married to me."

"Tell me," said Lee Denby, who was editor of the newspaper in Scott. "I've been interested before this, Dr. Alster, from a word said now and then. Tonight Jane indicates that you have been stationed in places other than the Midwest and northern California."

"I have been," said Alster, and said no more.

"Oh, come on now," protested Kate Beetz. "Unless you're a fugitive from something."

"I am at this minute trying to escape the prying curiosity of what I thought were my friends."

They all laughed, but Hilda persisted. Would Jane tell them?

"I went to medical school," said Alster dryly. "I completed my training. I have worked hard, but without distinction."

"Oh, no, you don't!" cried Jane. "He has always been chief of staff, or chief of surgical service. He has moved around a bit. That interests him."

"We know you had been married before Jane," said Louis Hunter.

Alster looked across at Jane, who was seated deep in a chair. She wore a long silk robe over her swimsuit. Her feet were bare. Her blond hair was twisted into a little bun on top of her head.

"Go on and tell them," he challenged her.

"All right, I will," said Jane. "Let's see. He graduated from medical school and was surgical resident in a large hospital. By then he was about twenty-four or twenty-five. And, as was natural, he married and had a son."

"As was natural," drawled Alster.

"That's when we first met Murphy Anderson," said Jane.

"We?" murmured Hilda.

"I was beginning my nurse's training. You knew that I was an RN?"

"I've heard you say so."

"But you don't always believe what I say."

"Girls, girls," Louis Hunter protested. "How are we going to get a rundown on Alster's past if you go cat-fighting on the fence?"

"Who's cat-fighting?" asked Jane. "We met up with

Murphy. He wasn't much older than Alster."

"Two years, three months, and five days," said Alster, who lay with his eyes closed.

"Murphy was as handsome and interesting then as he is now," said Jane. "Every female in the place was after him. But he was all doctor. Unfortunately he was in charge of the class that was guiding—"

"Trying to guide," murmured Alster.

"Trying to guide the interns and residents under him. There inevitably were conflicts with the younger men who, of course, knew all there was to know."

"No doctor knows as much medicine as he does the first year he's out of med school," Alster agreed.

"Yes," said Jane. "So Alster, like the other men, would often disagree with Murph, or he would have a real beef against one of them. Of course, his position guaranteed that he'd be right in any staff meeting."

"I recognized the edge he had on me," drawled Alster. "So I got mad about the situation, and I quit. Wife, small child, me. We went into private practice. And I flopped."

"Oh, he did not," said Jane. "He was building a good clientele."

"Hoo-hoo!" cried Cliff Doty.

"I was his office nurse," said Jane. "So I should know."

"Let me tell this part," said Alice Denby. "You couldn't get anywhere with Murphy Anderson, so you took out after Alster."

"And won him," purred Jane. "His wife had already left him, and taken their son."

"And he married you; you had a daughter two weeks later, and you've lived happily ever since," said Doty.

"If I told you the truth you wouldn't believe it."

94

"And you wouldn't let me use your pool any more, would you?" asked Cliff.

Alster got up out of his chair. "I am interested as all hell," he said, "in the story of my life as you all are making it up. But I have hospital rounds to make. So good night all. There's beer in the frig at a dollar a can."

He went into the house and could be seen going upstairs.

The group lingered, and talked about many things, but they were gone when Alster returned from the hospital. He went straight up to bed. Jane was sleeping in the guest room, a thing she often did when something had upset her.

"It's your own fault," he said, coming to the door of her room. "One day you will learn to keep your mouth shut."

"Are you angry?"

"Oh, no. Just tired." He went back to his own bed.

He was tired, but he did not sleep. He watched the blowing treetops shadowed against the glass wall of his room. He got up to walk about, find something to read, and he looked down on the dark gleam of the swimming pool. The chairs were as they had stood when he left the group for the hospital. The chaise on which he had lain, the four or five chairs, a cushion. Everything exactly as it had been. He could imagine the people. Jane in her long robe, Alice Denby entirely too bulbous to wear a bathing suit, her rather pompous, though knowledgeable, husband, Lee. What would the story of that couple be? Hilda, who proudly claimed that she had never been to a beauty parlor—and looked it. Kate, who was a great girl, but who should wear slacks always because of the broken blood vessels in her legs.

Wheee! Had these friends been as critical of him? Of Jane?

And what had Jane told them? What if he had stayed and let her tell the story, throwing in his bits of jeering derision, his word or two, perhaps, of vindication, even of pride?

How would it have gone?

He returned to the bed, stacked pillows so that he could see as much of the trees and the night sky as was possible, and began to think the story of Dr. Alster as it had happened, and as it might have been told. Jane fantasizing, he holding the thing down, perhaps beneath the border of truth. That was the way things usually were between them.

He had married Jane—he remembered. He remembered what she was like then, a gay, pretty girl—very pretty—and as forceful as she was today! What she wanted she usually got, fair means or foul. And she had wanted marriage with Alster.

"She took out after me," he probably would have said. "What chance did I have?"

So—they were married. Not the pretty flower and ribbon wedding he had known with his first bride. They had been married in the church; he was firm about not wanting a justice of the peace wedding, and they had gone to the small city where he had bought the practice of a man who had died suddenly. He shared an office with another doctor, a pediatrician, and they had the prospect of building up a good practice between them. Alster worked hard, and he was shocked when the local hospital refused him staff privileges after the first year, and his partner suggested that he have a separate office in a separate building. Margaret was six months old then, and he had explained that he could not, as a surgeon, work without a hospital. Jane argued with him, and in arguing revealed her poor relationship with his partner and with the town itself. So he must seek some other means of practicing and earning a living for his son, whom he supported, and Margaret. Jane would have to go back to work, but she never had done that.

How would she have told all this tonight to their friends around the swimming pool?

She would have said that Alster had not liked private practice—though he really had liked it, and would have enjoyed success in it. She would have glossed over that interlude and gone on to the Indian service years, which (he had heard her do it before) she made a romantic thing of sunsets and bright colors, Maria pottery and Navajo rugs. The artists of Taos, Katchina dolls, and the concerts of Indian music. She claimed that she had learned to sand paint. She had tried, and in doing so she had worked up a dangerous scandal with the young Indian who had risked his own position in the tribe by trying to teach her. Oh, there had been a fine fight!

All this had developed without Alster really being aware of what was happening. He liked the Southwest, he thought he was doing good work with the Indians. His income fixed, he could concentrate on preventive medicine, infant care, things of that sort. He himself liked the hot sun and the desert. He realized once in a while that Margaret was as brown as any Indian he cared for.

When the fight happened—Jane made a good story of that—"Blondes drive those men crazy"—he had protested hotly with her and urged the men to forgive her ignorance.

But the government had stepped in. Dr. Alster and his family must move elsewhere.

He was tempted to divorce Jane. He did not want to face a medical life of moving from one job to another. But the trauma of his first divorce still showed scars that could burn and shame him. That brief unfaithfulness had cost him his son and given him Jane in exchange. He still had Jane, who was what she had been then, a pretty woman sometimes, sometimes an exciting one. And he had Margaret, who was like a jewel, warm in his hands.

He would not lose this child. The loss of Michael had been very bad for him. Now they were friends, but—well, anyway—

He had asked for a year of freedom from his government contract. Yes, he probably would enter V.A. hospital service, but he wanted some perspective.

Now Jane made a romantic thing of this withdrawal from the human conflict. Then, she had loathed every day of it.

They had gone into the woods of northern Michigan, Jane fighting like a cat all the time. Now she told about it romantically. It certainly was a great change, the animals, the weather, the efforts to feed themselves, to build a log cabin, to survive at the bare level of existence.

And it had not worked. They both were essentially civilized people. Margaret must go to school. Alster must work at his profession: he must have books. Jane said she must have a flush toilet.

So he applied for a V.A. appointment, and got it. They moved about, filling in where a surgeon was needed. Alster studied and attended seminars. But he was content wherever they lived.

That was when he drew up rules for Jane. She was to attend to their daughter and to her duties as wife and homemaker. His lecture was specific and it reached her enough so that she spent a few subdued years, afraid of what might happen.

What did happen, after a time, was the four-year full assignment at the mental hospital in Missouri, where they assembled a proper home, made good friends, and Alster did good work. Jane was not too different from the other doctors' wives, and she was still trying to become what she called a civilized person. "That back to nature bit scared hell out of me!" she told the story. Usually her listeners laughed, though it really was no exaggeration. She had been frightened.

They decided to send Margaret to a good school. Michael recommended it, and himself was attending a seminary close enough to supervise things. Now he was about to be ordained and no longer would be in close touch, but Alster hoped that Margaret was firmly on the right track. It was hard to tell. The holidays spent at home could produce some startling things. But she loved her father passionately, and seemed to understand Jane.

It was during the V.A. years that Murphy Anderson again came into their lives. He was a government inspector, and regularly visited with the Alsters. He heard from Jane about the Indians, and about the deep woods. Alster would not speak freely of either period.

But he had liked that hospital job, the pretty town, the people with whom he worked. He was glad to have Murphy for a friend, to see him at regular intervals. It had surprised both men when the cholesterol experiment blew up in their faces. Though before it did, Murphy had suggested the California position to Alster, first as an assistant to Dr. Anderson, who was filling the position that Alster now held. But, at that time,

Alster decided against a move. Things were progressing fairly smoothly for him and Jane. Of course there were incidents—Jane sometimes made amusing stories about those times. Once, through Jane's indiscreet remarks, Alster was unfairly blamed for some trouble in the hospital. A patient, needing an emergency pneumothorax, had died because Alster, the surgeon, was out of town.

He was called on the carpet and bluntly asked if his wife had anything to do with his absence.

This angered Alster and infuriated Jane. He must resign at once, she said.

But he did not. He was innocent. He could prove that he had been granted leave, that his leave permission had not been recorded, and he was vindicated. Later he found that Jane had appealed to Murphy, who had refused his help.

"If I get him out of this, you might not like the way I do it," Murphy had told her.

"And if I don't like it," she had promised, "you'll go down with him!" There were things she could tell, she said, and expose Murphy.

That was a very touchy, bad spot in their lives. Murphy had traveled halfway across the country to find out what had happened and would happen.

He decided that Alster was innocent of neglect or abandonment of a patient. He had told Jane to let the man alone. Alster needed to defend himself, and he would do a better job of it if Jane stayed out of the matter.

Furious at him, she had hurled all sorts of accusations at Murphy, even the accusation that Alan's "trouble" was inherited.

Tonight would she have told their new friends about the boy, Alan? How could she, and be witty?

Back then it had sufficed that Alster was innocent, and Murphy's presence was coincidental, and routine. They had long known each other. Murphy was not needed, Alster could clear himself and did so. This was his job, and he did it.

But, afterward, the Alsters were not so popular as they had been. Jane talked too much—and Alster himself began to drink. Too much.

"He still needs and gets his regular nip," she possibly would have told their friends tonight, most of whom knew of the bottle he kept in his desk drawer. Though, with his work going very well, and his home life fairly calm, he opened that drawer less frequently.

Alster thought he knew the whole story; Jane thought she did; and now the version she had given their friends would color this life here in Baumgarten.

Probably Murphy Anderson was the only one to know the entire truth. He knew when to talk, when not. He had advised Alster to make friends here in this post. He had said, correctly, that every man needed a friend or two, and he seemed destined to be Alster's. In return, Murphy's "friend" should work at the job. He thought he was doing just that, though Jane had given him some argument on the subject. And both Murphy and her husband had assured *her* that friends were a necessity.

"You have a young daughter coming along, and she will need the background of friendliness."

Murphy did not like or trust Jane, so he talked to Alster privately about that. "I am not going to tell you what to do about Jane—" he said musingly.

"Strangling isn't legal in this state."

"No. No, it isn't. And you must love her, or you did love her once."

"Passion," Alster had amended.

"All right, passion. You gave up what might have been a very good life for one with Jane. And it's getting late in the day, my friend, to start out on still another one. It was wise to send Margaret away to school."

"I sometimes wonder about that."

"I'm right."

"You aren't, always."

"Nor you."

And, being men, they left things at that. Jane probably did not. She disliked Murphy and tried to conceal it. He knew too much of the truth about her and about Alster himself. But they had come here to Baumgarten on his advice.

And her behavior up to now might be a striking out at Murphy, who had bought them here. Perhaps she was ready to build on this. If so, Alster must stop her. Tonight he should have stayed down there with the group.

But now he had better go to sleep. Even the moon was behind the mountain. He let two of the pillows slip down from the bed and slid under the quilt.

Michael was to be ordained in the summer—Jane said ordained priest, but of course it was only deacon. He was a brilliant boy, had taken his first college degree at nineteen. Alster was going to his son's ordination; Margaret would. But Jane? Probably not. She disliked being a background person, and would not want to pose as Michael's mother. His real mother had now been dead for three years.

Jane probably was counting on the fact that now they no longer would need to spend money on Michael. She probably had things planned for that money. But so did Alster. Oh, there would be a fine argument but he was planning on investing those hundreds of dollars.

And Alster himself? He was still a young man as doctors went.

He knew his professional needs, and he knew what he could do in this good job. He looked much as he had when he had loved and been loved. By Alice, by Jane.

There had been problems, there would be others. But as for himself—he would try—knowing that he probably could handle what might come. If he wanted to. The big thing was—to—want to—

The next morning, Jane, downstairs with his breakfast ready—this did not always happen—asked what he was going to do about the straw boss.

"The fellow in veneers?"

"If he is making trouble . . ."

"He hasn't made any. And unless he does I am not going to do anything."

"Can I keep your records?"

"No."

"Why not?"

"Because I want to do it myself. You see, Jane, there isn't work enough here for two doctors."

"Now, see here, Alster!"

He waited, eating his grapefruit with precision. "Some days I am excessively busy," he said, "but there are gaps. No doctor is overworked with only three or four hundred patients. Most of them healthy."

"I hope you don't say anything like that to Pemscot."

"Only when I point out to him that my research project will fill my time, so that I won't be tempted to leave, as Murphy did."

"I thought he left because of something Alan had

done." She set his eggs before him.

"He didn't. He wanted to work with people again. And have freedom. That's why he left the government service."

"Would you be idiot enough to do that?"

He smiled. "Last night," he said, "I decided that I was any kind of idiot you could define. May I have some toast?"

5

This having been decided and announced, the Alsters settled down to the environment in which they found themselves. Alster was interested in his research, and in addition to it, he found that there was enough work in this hospital to keep both himself and Joe busy. When needed, or not, their friends thought up diversions of one sort or another.

Helen Cobb lost her voice, and Alster was sure she had some sort of throat problem. She smoked a lot and he told her to stop, which she did when around Alster or Jane. "Don't stop on my account," Jane advised. "Alster doesn't tell me about his patients. I don't report on them to him."

But she did ask her husband about Helen.

"I don't know," he said. "She is frightened about cancer, and she won't let me do a biopsy of the node I finally was allowed to find on her larynx."

"Oh, Alster!"

"I know. They are friends. That is, we see a lot of them. I have not liked Helen especially. But she is a patient, too, Jane, and as such—"

"What can you do?"

At first he did not answer. He did not trust Jane with much information about his patients. "I think," he said, "that I'll tell Dan to take her to some expensive clinic or specialist."

Jane smiled at him. "Will that impress her?"

"It will impress Dan, and he'll make her have the surgery she certainly must have."

"Good *night!*" said Jane. "I can't imagine Helen Cobb without a voice."

"Don't talk about it. You could ruin my plan."

"She has a right to fear cancer, hasn't she?"

"So do we all."

He worked on the Cobb case, and saw them off to the clinic he had recommended. That kept him busy, what with the usual run of accidents, a fishhook in a man's eyelid, routine examinations.

"But no old people," he said to Joe Raithel one morning. "I knew something was missing around here. We have no arthritis, or old-age malnutrition—"

"Because we have only employees and their families as patients. By the time they break hips and develop acute osteoarthritis, they are retired."

Alster nodded. "You're right. Of course Anderson has some . . ."

"Over in Scott? Sure he does. My mother goes to him, and she won't listen to a thing I tell her."

Alster laughed. "Treating one's own family isn't profitable business, Joe."

"I guess not. But I'll have to keep myself brushed up on geriatrics for when I move on from here, won't I?"

Alster's head went up. "You're thinking of leaving?"

"My contract runs until July. But I would like to stay on as assistant if you'd care to have me. This place lets me be with my mother and do things for my brother."

"How is he getting along?"

Joe shrugged. "He seems to be in regression. For

how long—who knows?"

"Well, keep your name on your parking space. Let's go look at our hernia case."

So the Alsters did have friends. Some they liked better than others, but they managed to get along with most of them. Murphy continued to come around. There, too, he and Alster were friends, though they often disagreed on some point or another. These friends stuck together, helped, and abused one another, but in all cases they relied on each other. The dinner group especially demonstrated how this worked. They could separate widely on something as silly as whether fresh spinach did or did not make good green salad, and draw together into a firm group when not wanting Rose Oquest brought to one, or several, Friday night dinners. But Eric Pemscot was boss man of the project. These were points to be considered in a group, and decided upon.

Theirs was an exclusive group, though Murphy was always welcome. Cliff Doty decided that Murphy should take Oquest off their hands.

"Why not you?" asked Jane. "You're single."

"For my own reasons."

"I think Murphy has reasons, too."

This brightened interest. The Alsters had known Dr. Anderson . . .

Dr. Alster lifted his hands. "Jane and I," he said firmly, "see nothing, hear nothing, and speak nothing."

"Jane, too?" asked Hilda in mock disbelief.

"If she doesn't, don't call the coroner. It will be a case of justified wife-beating."

Jane laughed. "I've heard that before," she said.

"And have the scars to prove it?" asked Hilda.

"A few," said Jane.

So, in this strange way, the group held together, friends to a degree. "Maybe all friends are that way," Alster told Murphy, "with concessions made, and reservations advisable."

"Marriages are that way."

"Of course they are. I've completed my first month of cholesterol tests if you would care to look at the results."

Murphy took the big book and looked up at Alster. "Who's keeping the records?"

"I am."

"Why not Jane?"

"Oh, I have the time . . ."

"If you do these late at night."

"No, really, Murph, there's not work enough here . . ."

"I know how much work there is. How it can come on you in gobs of o.r. duty and then a day or two of empty office chairs. I've wondered what made you look so gant lately."

Alster had an obscene word for "gant."

"You'd do better to keep busy in the hospital; Jane would do better if she had something like these records . . ."

Alster flared. "Look!" he cried. "Don't tell me what to do! Nor what Jane should be doing!"

Murphy leaned back in the chair, tipping it at a dangerous angle. "I always have told you," he said quietly. "And I can promise you, my friend, that I won't take over your research come the nervous breakdown."

Alster stared at him, then shrugged. "All right," he said. "Jane will think she's won the fight she's been making."

"Let her think so. How are you two doing, by the way?"

Alster took the record book and set it to one side; he would take it to Jane that evening. "We're like dogs," he said. "We have tramped down the rough spots, and finally are making a nest for ourselves in the tall grass."

"Jane, too?"

"Oh, yes, as she's always done. Her talk, her exaggerations, are becoming recognized, and so tolerated."

"She's a smart dame."

"She is."

And so things were going when an executive from the main offices came to visit the Baumgarten Complex; and a party was given in his honor, the hosts being the heads of the various departments. This got Alster into a dinner coat and Jane into a beautiful dress of gauzelike pink stuff, set off by a wide pink satin sash, the ends of which trailed to the floor. Zipping up the back of the gown before they left for the club, Alster told her the dress was too tight. A size too small, maybe?

"I have a good figure, Doctor."

"Yes, you do. But be careful what you eat tonight. One noodle may be too much."

"Are they going to have noodles?"

"I wouldn't be sure that they are not."

So they went to the party and Jane's dress, as she had hoped, was a sensation. It really was beautiful and Alster determined to ask, later, how she had acquired it.

She flirted prettily with the visiting official, and then turned her attention to Murphy Anderson. She sat beside him at the dinner and insisted that he dance with her afterward.

"You know I'm no dancer, Jane," he protested.

But she persisted, and rather than make a scene, he led her out upon the floor. And at the first turn, the zipper of her beautiful dress gave way.

Murphy stopped dead in the middle of the floor. "For God's sake!" he cried. "Don't you have anything on under this dress?"

Jane was too horrified to speak. Murphy reached out his hand to catch Kate Beetz who was dancing past with the guest of honor. "Help me!" he cried.

And Kate laughed. Everyone laughed. Murphy took off his jacket and put it around Jane's shoulders. "I'll take you home," he said.

"You will not!" She was so furious at him, at the expensive dress, too cheaply made, at Alster for having told her it was too small . . .

"Don't you have another dress at home?" Murphy persisted.

Hilda Curren came to his aid. "I'll take over, Murphy," she said, though she was laughing, too. "That's what happens when you have new clothes. Mine are so old they are tried and true."

"Where's Alster?"

"Watching from the sidelines."

Everyone was watching. So Jane went with Hilda, down to the locker room, which served as ladies room, dressing room, and a dozen other functions at the club. Hilda was efficient, if brutal. "Don't you have a damn thing under this?" she asked, as Murphy had done.

"Panties," said Jane, beginning to weep.

"Oh, don't do that," said Hilda practically. "Let's see. I think—"

She found what she was looking for, a very large safety pin; and pulling the dress together at the waist so that she could pin it, she, too, said that Jane should have bought a size larger. Ignoring Jane's remarks on that subject, she found scissors and snipped the pink satin sash free. This she drew around Jane's throat, tied it in a loose knot, and let it hang down her back.

"Now," she said, "you must tell your dancing partner to hold it in place. Me, if this happened to me—well, for one thing I wear a slip, and for another, I know enough to buy my clothes big enough . . ."

"And for another, you never had a dress like this in all your life," snapped Jane. She started up the stairs.

"Where'd you find that wife of yours?" Hilda asked Alster when he thanked her for helping Jane. "In a bumblebee's nest?"

Alster looked across the dance floor; Jane was again dancing with Murphy, being very gay about the whole episode. And the tall doctor, having recovered his jacket, was being kind to her. She must have been dreadfully humiliated. And Murphy was a kind man, which he later was to regret.

Dr. Anderson was not really a member of the dinner group, but the next Friday evening Jane invited him to come as the Alsters' guest.

He enjoyed the company, and he went. But he was not prepared to have Jane kiss him when he arrived, to sit next to him, and to devote the evening to him.

Of course everyone was still laughing about the dress episode and Alster's declaration that someone else was buying Jane's clothes. He would never pay for a dress like that! And then there was the question of whether she did or did not have anything on under it.

Kate Beetz said that she had promised to write the visiting official when the matter was resolved. "It simply made the evening," she declared.

Murphy, Jane said, was the only one ready to forget the matter and be kind to her. She was grateful. What could she do for him?

"Hey!" he said to Alster, coming into his office late one afternoon. "What's got into Jane?"

"I've noticed," said Alster.

"Well, call her off, will you? I like to come to your house, but lately she snuggles."

"That's what I've noticed," said Alster.

"That night, at the dance, I lent her my coat. You stood ten feet away, laughing. I think you even buttoned your jacket."

Alster was laughing again. "There's more," he said.

Murphy groaned, and went to look out at the view offered by the glass wall. Two jays were fighting over a piece of bread. "What more?" he asked.

"Well, she thinks you took her side against me in the keeping of my records for the cholesterol project. I told her the day after the dance that she was to do it. I thought telling her then would be a diversion."

"Was it?"

"Only partially. Because I assured her that I was going to keep an eagle eye out to be sure the records were accurate."

"But she must have known that you would . . ."

"Yes, but I *told* her. And she asked me if I didn't trust her."

"And you said that you did not."

"I said that I never had trusted her."

"Well, she must have known that, too."

"She did, she does. But the trouble is, Joe Raithel overheard our conversation. We were here in the office, and he was coming in to tell me something. He took the matter seriously, and now you have competition with him. He assured Jane that I was joking, that she was a capable girl, et cetera, et cetera. And she asked him to carry the bulky record book up to the house for her."

Murphy grunted. "May the best man win!" he said.

"And you hope it won't be you."

"Alster—"

"I know. Jane's put you over these hurdles before, and I've handled it."

"How are the tests going?"

Alster told him, and when they left the hospital they found neither Jane nor Dr. Raithel in the house. Nor was dinner being prepared. Alster swore.

He and Murphy went to the club for dinner, and when he came home, having made rounds and done some chart work, Jane was in bed asleep. She was still asleep when he went to the hospital in the morning, disliking but determined to have a showdown with Miss Jane. The price of that damned dress, the cold kitchen when he brought a friend home . . .

He ate breakfast at the hospital, and went on to o.r. Joe had better be there before him, and he was. So Alster settled down to the cyst they were about to remove. A routine bit of surgery, which went well. The patient could be sent to his room and bed.

"Dr. Alster," said Joe, as his superior was shedding his gown, cap, and gloves, "could I talk to you?"

"Sure. So talk." Alster accepted the chart board from the nurse.

"In private, I think."

Alster's black eyebrows went up, but he nodded.

"Will my office do?" he asked, more intent on what he was writing than on Joe's problems. They could be important; they could be infinitesimal.

This one was—well—annoying. Joe began by saying that he and Jane had had dinner with his mother the night before. "She gets lonesome."

"Women her age do, often," said Dr. Alster.

"I'm talking about Jane."

Dr. Alster swung his chair to face his young assistant. "Now, why on earth should you think . . . ?" he began.

"I am puzzled myself," said Joe. "You know, I interrupted yesterday when you were talking to your wife."

Alster shut his eyes, trying to remember.

"And I got the impression—well, could I ask, without offending you, if you two don't like each other?"

Alster stared at him, then he laughed. The chap was so damned *young!* But he was being honest; he *was* puzzled.

"Well," said Alster, picking up a pencil, spanning it between his thumb and forefinger, "we've been married seventeen years, Raithel."

"Yes, I know. But—"

"That predicates mutual attraction, doesn't it?"

"Yes, I would say so."

"The important thing is, and I do think Jane would agree, we know each other, intimately and completely. And that *is* important." But he could tell that he had not completely answered Dr. Raithel's question.

"I would have to be liked," said the young man, his tone troubled. "Or loved, I guess that's what I mean."

"You will find your place in life," the older doctor assured him, "and like the rest of us learn all you'll need to know about it."

Alster gazed out at the trees, blowing in a stiff wind.

"Do you remember, Joe," he asked, "the time when I was in Sacramento or some place and you had a poison case come in? A child who had got into his mother's birth-control pills. You were fighting valiantly to save the little fellow and were grateful when I walked in, knowing what to do. Afterward you said you were shocked that *you* had not known what to do, and I asked you if you remembered being taught anything specifically on that subject when you were in medical school."

"And I said, 'No.'"

"You said 'no,' and I said that I had not been either. Over the years, I had to learn what to do. As a surgeon, my impulse was always to operate, which is nearly always a mistake. But I learned. I studied the poison center in every city where I worked. I always establish one in my hospitals. I showed you what we had here."

"A bottle of ipecac, and twenty-five grams of activated charcoal? That's a poison center?"

"I've since added some stickers that say in bright green letters 'Mr. Yuk,' which I give to mothers to put on dangerous medicine bottles in their homes."

"We should be trained."

"We should be. And, if not, we should be patient and learn from experience."

Joe grinned weakly. "Thank you, sir."

If, during the morning, Alster gave the matter any thought, it was to suppose that Joe Raithel would resume his attentions to Jane, a practice that he had somewhat avoided after the graffiti episodes. There were those who decided that Dr. Alster had told him to "lay off." Actually, he had said very little. He just might have to now.

This thought annoyed him but was immediately dispelled when word came in, about one o'clock that same day, that Joe's brother, sick for several years with leukemia, had suddenly died.

The news came at a rather bad time. Some woodsman had been hurt and was being brought to the hospital. But Alster told the agitated young doctor that he must, of course, go immediately to his mother, and then on to Sacramento.

"I'm sure Charles's doctor did something wrong!" declared Joe, looking as if he might fly off in all directions.

"Wait until you know just what happened," said Alster, seeing the ambulance coming down the hill from the woods. "Maybe you should take a mild sedative, and remember that you have your mother to think of."

"I know. I will— Oh, how can I leave if you have an amputation?"

"I'll manage," said Alster. If the excited fellow would just take his jitters and *leave!* He was sorry of course, that the brother had died, but death had to have been expected. And just now Alster had some things to do besides counseling a hysterical young man, who should have kept better control of himself.

He said as much to the o.r. crew, which he probably should not have done. But here he was with a skull fracture and other problems. An hour or two would not have made any difference. The brother was already dead. "Of course, Joe was a basket case," he reminded himself, aloud.

"I wonder if Mrs. Alster has heard," said someone in scrub, and this turned Alster to ice.

"Would you care to break scrub and ask her?" he asked.

"I'm sorry, Doctor."

"We are all sorry. I am for blowing my cool. I know Dr. Raithel was shocked and out of control. But, for

God's sake, let's forget it for the rest of the afternoon, and take care of this man. Will someone light the X-ray screen, *please*?"

Naturally, word spread about the hospital and the plant that Dr. Alster had indeed "blown his cool." It was, perhaps, justified. He had put in a good six hours caring for a badly injured man, doing the work of two doctors. He considered sending for Murphy, but later said he hadn't had time to think of anything but that mashed-in skull and that fractured collarbone and arm.

"What was your reaction," asked Murphy, who knew Alster well, "when they came around with a collection for flowers?"

Alster stared at him. "I don't remember their doing that," he said blankly. And Murphy laughed.

Alster was not free to go to the funeral, which was held on the second morning after the death. Jane went, looking demurely beautiful in a tailored black suit and a white silk blouse, a small hat on her head. This meant a long drive, and the carful of people left very early in the morning. They returned late in the afternoon.

The day had turned misty and sometimes rainy. Jane was tired and Alster late coming in for dinner. But she had food prepared, and talked a little about the trip. She didn't care for funerals, she said.

"Very few people do," Alster assured her. He said yes, he had been busy, and hoped things could be quiet that night.

And the door chimes sounded.

Jane was not quite finished in the kitchen, so he went to answer, entirely surprised to find Joe Raithel's mother on his doorstep.

She announced herself as Mrs. Raithel; Alster supposed that he had met the woman before, but he had no memory of her. She was a small, round person, and she said that perhaps she should not have bothered the doctor. But she wanted to get through with this awful day. Charles, she said, was her son, as well as Joseph's brother, but Charles also had a wife and two children. "That pushes a mother into the background," she said.

Alster was charming to her. He took her raincoat and led her to a seat on the couch, across from the little fire on the living-room hearth.

Jane came in and asked Mrs. Raithel how she had got there. "I thought perhaps you had stayed in Sacramento."

"I have a little car," said Joe's mother, laying back a series of scarfs and the edges of her suit coat. "I came back to Scott from Sacramento on the stage."

"The bus," murmured Alster. "Would you like a glass of wine, Mrs. Raithel?"

She flushed a little. "I would rather have tea," she said.

"Have you had dinner?"

"I ate something on the road during a rest stop. That was about four o'clock. I'll fix myself some Cream of Wheat when I get home."

Jane made the tea and brought it, a small glass pot, a cup, sugar and cream on a small tray. Alster placed a table to hold it.

"I shouldn't be keeping you," said the poor woman. "And I'll get going quite soon." She drank some tea, gratefully. Jane looked questioningly at the doctor.

"She's all right," he said. "She's had a hard day and we'll see that she gets home and to bed. I can't understand why Joe . . ."

"Oh, yes!" said Mrs. Raithel. "I know why I came. You know, Charles, the son we buried today, has been sick for a long time. And yesterday his wife asked me—she said she meant to ask Joe, but he had gone out on some errand—something about whether Charles used a handkerchief in the pocket of his suit. I don't believe in open coffins, do you?" She looked up at Dr. Alster.

"No," he said, "I don't." He rose and refilled her teacup. "Just take your time, Mrs. Raithel," he said.

"You are being very kind."

Why shouldn't he be? But what in the devil did the woman want? He resumed his seat near her.

"I don't like all these open windows, do you?" she asked, looking about the room.

"It's like living in the woods. We find the effect restful."

"Well, that's good. Joe could have had an apartment in the complex, but I decided I would like living in town better. And Julia said she didn't want to worry any longer about the kids getting hold of the pills and things, so she wanted Joe—" She broke off to pick up her purse, a large one, from the floor beside her chair. She opened it and took out a plastic bag fastened with a Twistum; it appeared to contain several boxes and little bottles—she held this out to Dr. Alster.

"I told Julia that I would give them to Joe, but I forgot to do it."

"What is it?" asked Dr. Alster, juggling the bag in his hand.

"Oh, these are the medicines Charles had been taking. He took all sorts of pills and things, and they are very expensive. I thought you should have them, that you probably could use them. They cost so much, and the children shouldn't have them around, and I really shouldn't, either. I take some pills, thyroid, and something for blood pressure, and aspirin now and then. I might get mixed up, so I thought these would be safer with you."

Alster nodded, and laid the bag on the table behind him. "I'll put them into the clinic," he said. "As you say, medicines are very expensive."

"Yes, they are. For a time, we hoped they would help Charles. But they didn't seem to."

"A great deal of research is being done on leukemia," said Dr. Alster.

"Yes, sir, I know. Joe studied about it; he was devoted to his brother. You know, he would go down to see him on his free days, and he wanted to give him his personal care but, of course, he could not bring Charles to your hospital, though he might have stayed with me, but Julia would not let him. She—well, I must be getting home." She struggled to get up, and Alster offered her a hand.

"Am I to understand?" asked Alster, "that Joe let you come home by yourself on the bus?"

"Yes. He is staying with Julia until the first of the week. He—"

Abruptly Alster went to the far end of the room. "Can you give me Julia's telephone number?" he asked.

"Alster . . ." said Jane warningly.

"Well, he's needed here, Jane. He knows that! I am just about swamped, and I expect him to come back and be on duty tomorrow morning. He has done what he could for his brother; now his job needs him here."

He was very angry, showed it, and his anger frightened Mrs. Raithel. She said she should be leaving, and Jane agreed. She helped her into the raincoat, thanked her for the drugs, and went with her out to the car.

"I felt like going with her," she told Alster when she

came back into the room. "The poor woman, driving off into the night, with her grief for her son . . ."

"The idea of Joe letting her come home alone on the stage!"

"Perhaps he didn't know she was leaving."

"He told her he would stay with Julia until the first of the week, didn't he?"

"Yes, he did, but I really think you should tone down a little. Did you reach him?"

"The phone was busy. But I'll get him back tomorrow. I mean to go to the club dinner and eat it in peace and a fine aura of Chivas Royale, while Joe takes over his own job at the hospital. Though, with my luck, he won't get in so much as an ingrown toenail. But you count on me for that dinner. *You count on it!*"

Jane supposed he got Joe back and at work, because he came home in plenty of time to dress and go to the club for dinner that Friday night. The skies had cleared, and someone had brought flowers for the center of the table. The menu included giant crab legs, he was told, and that set him up still further.

"What's got into Alster?" Kate asked Jane.

"Oh, he's had a rough week at the hospital, and he's reacting. He'll settle down."

"I hope not," said Kate. "This is fun. He— Oh, my goodness, look who just came in."

Jane looked. Everyone looked. For, with Murphy Anderson behind her, in came Rose Oquest, looking like a million dollars and conscious of the furor she was creating.

"I thought she was Pemscot's girl," murmured Jane.

"I could find an answer for that," said Kate.

"Come on! Say it! She's anybody's girl."

"Watch out for Alster."

"He calls her Oquist, and she hates it."

"But does she hate him?"

"She had better," said Jane grimly.

"Oh, gee, gosh!" said Kate. Jane turned. "What . . . ?"

"They've brought the boy."

"Alan? Well, Murphy does, sometimes. I mean, they've come to our home . . ."

"I know. And he brought him to the complex's kids' party at Christmas time. The boy hit the *piñata* so hard the pole came down on another kid's head and three stitches were needed."

"But Alan had a whale of a time."

"Indeed he did. He can be rather appealing."

The Alan in question was indeed, at times, rather appealing. Somewhat autistic, he had long been a problem for Murphy. Of course he knew the Alsters, and they knew him. This night he made straight for Jane and asked her if she knew "Dad's new girl friend."

"Isn't she pretty?"

"Yes, she is," said Jane. "Are you going to eat with them, or do you want to sit with Mrs. Beetz and me?"

Kate made warning sounds.

Alan glanced at her. He was a slender boy and wore round, black-rimmed glasses with thick lenses. "I don't want to sit with you, either," he said. He turned back to Jane. "I'll sit with you, though."

"Well, do as you want. I think you'll have to decide. The people are finding their places."

Alan ran off, and Kate had things to say to Jane. She was, she said, afraid of the boy.

"He isn't dangerous, Kate."

"He does some pretty wild things."

"He gets out of control. But he's smart. He can learn.

Murphy has a real problem, of course."

"His friend Rose isn't afraid of the kid. For heaven's sake!"

Rose Oquest had taken Alan's arm and was leading him to a chair between her and Murphy. She was talking to him in an exaggeration of help and concern.

"You'd think he was three," murmured Jane.

If Alan didn't want crab legs, Rose was sure the cook would find him a hamburger.

Murphy spoke quietly to the boy, and he settled down. The waitress brought him a bowl of chili, earlier provided for. Alan began to eat it hungrily, and from then on, he ignored Rose.

"I get the distinct impression that was Rose's idea. I understand she has an eye on one of our unmarried men."

"She won't get one," said Kate.

"Oh, she might. She's good looking, and men seem to like her. I will say, Kate, she is always exquisitely dressed."

"She works for a dress shop. I think they feel she is a good advertisement."

"Good Lord!" cried Alster. "You women have a solution for everything."

"No, we don't," Jane told him. "For instance, which one of our men will Rose get?"

Alster busied himself with a crab leg."

"And if you can't answer that," said Kate, "tell me why the available men should seek elsewhere. With me and Hilda available."

Alster laughed, and together they made a gay thing of pairing off the available members. Noticeably leaving Murphy, and Rose, and the now-sleepy boy out of the discussion, and the ones that followed.

Murphy noticed it, and at least once he seemed to

123

suggest to Rose that they leave. But she shook her head. She really was a handsome woman. That evening she was wearing a well-fitting pants suit of bronze-gold silk, a scarf tied about her throat in a way that Kate and Jane agreed they could never achieve.

"It looks like a bandage," growled Alster, and that made their group laugh aloud.

Rose leaned toward Judge Lawrence. Had the company, she asked, her voice clear, really been able to buy the patch of ground owned by someone she called "Old Pigeon"?

Murphy protested. It was not cricket, he told her, to talk business at these gatherings.

"But I am not a company man," Rose retorted, "and I need not follow your rules."

Judge smiled at her gently. "But I do," he reminded her.

"I know Pigeon," said Rose. "He has maybe a hundred acres of beautiful, uncutover trees, with water—I understand it was once a placer mine."

"It's still supposed to pan a little gold," said Cliff Doty.

"Oh, let's go there sometime," cried Jane enthusiastically.

"Pigeon lets people," said Rose. "But that's off if he sells the acreage. He really should. He must be eighty years old."

"He'd sell it," said Alster thoughtfully, wiping his fingers carefully on a large napkin. "And the company would bring in a sawmill."

"Why not?" demanded Rose. "At his age . . ."

"Is he starving?" asked Alster, his tone cold.

"Oh, I don't think so. He probably has some income."

"Then let the man alone," said Alster firmly. "By

God, maybe he thinks some trees should be allowed to die of old age."

Rose leaned toward him, her pretty chin cupped in her hand, her elbow on the table. "Dr. Richard Alster," she said sweetly, "are you quoting Thoreau again?"

"Would you know if I did?" he countered.

"The thing I do know," she replied, still in that clear, limpid voice, "is that sometimes you are a great bore."

His friends began to smile, to laugh, and then to roar with laughter.

Murphy spoke above the uproar; there was laughter in his eyes, too. "I've heard tell," he said, "that there is a place for everyone. Tonight, I think that Miss Oquest may have found hers."

Alster stood up. "I'm leaving, Jane," he said abruptly. "Are you coming with me?"

Se did rise and follow him; at the door, she turned and made a circle gesture to her friends with the tip of a finger and her thumb.

"I want to get some work done," Alster told her as they went into their house. "Do you have the test record book here?"

Alster was calling the hospital desk, locating himself.

"Of course," said Jane, "on the tray shelf in the kitchen. It's up to date."

The hospital reported that there had been no emergencies. Yes, Dr. Alster was on call. Dr. Raithel would be back in the morning.

Alster thanked the nurse on duty, and went to fetch the record book, saying that he wanted to add a check on the alpha levels of the people on his list. He was not sure the HLDS had been recorded.

"Yes, it has been," said Jane, who was opening and examining the bag of medicines that Mrs. Raithel had left behind. She set the boxes and little tubes of pills in a neat row, looking at each label as she drew it from the plastic sack. She had a frown between her eyes.

"What are you doing?" Alster asked.

"Oh, seeing what sort of junk we have here. I'm ready for bed. What about you?"

"I'll check this material first. You've had a long day."

"Yes, I really have." She swept the medicine containers back into the bag. "Good night, dear. The crab was good, wasn't it?"

Alster turned his cheek for her kiss, and continued to run his pencil point down a column on the page before him. Jane did keep good records.

The next day, Raithel was back, looking tired, and probably resentful about losing the weekend with his brother's family. Alster had spoken to him courteously, then discussed with him the case of the woodsman with the fractured skull, and outlined the day's obligations. "So far as we can follow them," he said. "I am getting the children's immunity records up to date. Parents forget booster shots, and newcomers often have not had measles. Well, anyway, we shall be busy."

He left the ward, and as he passed his office he slowed his step, surprised to think he saw Jane at the file drawers that lined a long wall. He was inclined to go in and ask her what she was doing there—then decided he could do that later. He had an accumulation of his own records in his office, a claim for a disability allowance for the injured man's family—and in all this busyness, he forgot about Jane. She probably was checking the HLDS records that he had mentioned to her last night. She had had a small notebook in her hand.

That evening when he came home he looked for,

then asked for, the medicines that Mrs. Raithel had brought.

"Why?" asked Jane. "Does Joe want them?"

"I don't believe he knows she brought them. We haven't talked much; we both had a busy day. But I would like to check them and see what can go into the clinic pharmacy supplies."

"I decided to throw them out," said Jane, turning bacon in a pan.

"Why did you do that?" asked Alster. "Do you want a martini?"

"The German wine, please, with dinner. Well, they looked like pretty strong stuff to me. And with young people here . . ."

Alster's head turned. "What young people?" he asked.

"Margaret. She's coming in tomorrow and bringing a friend."

"A girl?"

"I hope so. I thought you and I would use the twin bedroom."

"Why is she coming?"

"I think it's the end of spring term. She wrote to you a week ago for plane fare. I suppose you sent it."

"I called the airline and charged it to my account. Well, it will be fine to have her. Maybe we can take a couple of days and drive to the Oregon beaches."

"Maybe, but Margaret usually has her own plans."

"We get along."

"Yes, you do. She adores you. And wraps you around her finger with the greatest of ease."

6

The next day, Margaret did come. Alster drove to the airport to meet her and was relieved to find that she had come alone. But he asked about the guest. "I wanted to have a day or so alone with you first," said the pretty girl.

"Right around your finger," murmured Jane. Alster laughed and went off to claim his daughter's luggage.

She was a beautiful girl, he told himself. She had Jane's blond hair, perhaps a few shades darker, and she wore it loose, hanging to her shoulders. With this she had her father's dark eyes. The combination was smashing. Everyone thought so. Even in the jeans and bright red shirt, which she had chosen to wear for travel, every male eye in the airport followed her.

"Ah, to be sixteen again," sighed Jane.

"I'll be seventeen in three months," Margaret reminded her. "Do we have a long drive? Hey, aren't the woods gorgeous?"

"Wait till you see our house," Jane reminded her.

"Near the woods?"

"A birdhouse in one of the trees."

"Oh, thank you, Jesus!" said Margaret fervently.

Both Jane and Alster turned to look at her. She sat between them and reached a hand to the wheel.

"It's Eden," she sighed when Alster pulled up to the front door. "I am sure you commune."

"Do we?" Alster asked his wife. Margaret had jumped out of the car. She went all around the house, upstairs and down; she bent lovingly over the pool, and picked daisies from the flowers Jane labored so diligently to maintain in decorative array. Her parents watched her, uncertain smiles on their faces.

Alster carried her bags upstairs, and said they must be full of rocks.

"Books," trilled Margaret. "My Bibles weigh a lot."

"Your . . . . ?"

"I have all the translations," she said happily. "Besides Mark's King James, bound in leather. He bound it himself. He—"

"Who is Mark?" asked Alster.

"The man I love," said the girl, and went on talking as if no bomb had fallen. "Of course I love all men, but Mark is the special one."

"Bangladesh," murmured Jane as she handed Alster a napkin.

Alster relaxed. Yes, she had put them over the hurdles at various times. She had wanted them to ask their black maid's family to share their home, friends, and clothes. The maid, sensibly, had refused. Margaret wanted her parents to go back to Indian country, the Dakotas this time. At Christmas she had accepted, but protested, lavish gifts, saying they should send the money to the starving families of Bangladesh.

So they tried to accept and not protest what seemed to be a washing wave of religious fervor.

"It's not like our church . . ." Jane said the next morning. Margaret had come down early and was in the pool. "Going around telling me that Jesus would save me."

"Have you talked to her about it?"

"Not yet, but she's put all sorts of banners and posters in her room."

"Jane . . ."

"I told her that she must not tack or tape anything to the structure. So she's starting a sort of clothesline with the things hung on it, and we have to go in to the bus station at eleven."

"To meet the love of her life who binds his Bible in leather. Who *is* he, Jane?"

"I only know that his name is Mark."

"Where did she meet him, where does he live?"

"She met him at what she calls a student crusade. He says he is a saint, just as she is."

"Episcopal?"

"Baptist. She has been singing in the Baptist choir. They are more relaxed than the Episcopalians."

"Does Margaret have a voice?"

"She says we all have voices with which to praise the Lord."

Alster put down his coffee cup. "I am going to work," he said. "I just may never come home."

"Coward."

"I certainly am." He went out through the kitchen door.

"Bless you, Father," Margaret called from the pool.

Having reached his office, still looking dazed, he called Jane. What were they going to *do,* he asked. He told her what had happened, and vowed he was not going to be the subject of a benediction from his daughter.

Jane laughed, and sympathized with him.

"If that guy you pick up at the bus station has a beard and a white robe that says 'Jesus Saves,' refuse to bring him home."

"I shall, I shall!" she promised. "But, Alster—for one

thing, it is strange to ask me for advice, instead of passing out orders."

"I'm in a daze."

"So am I, frankly. But suppose we don't argue, or seem to criticize. We can try to go along with Margaret and handle each crisis, if any happen, as each arrives."

Alster guessed he could do that if Jane could. "Where's the fella going to sleep?"

"We'll arrange for that, too," she said.

And Alster put down the phone, ready to keep himself very busy at the hospital that day. "I usually want to spend as much time as possible with Margaret," he told himself sadly.

But he had to go home that afternoon, and he had to meet this Mark fella. The man's last name was Halloran. He was at least five years older than Margaret. His hair was thick, a light brown, he was smooth shaven, and he wore a white cable-knit cardigan sweater with a sash like a bathrobe's. But, well, no actual robe, beard, or sandals.

Alster nodded to Jane. He would try . . . the nod said, and he asked the young man if he would like a drink.

"Not alcoholic." The chap had a good voice.

Alster went for his own drink. "Definitely alcoholic," he told the ice-cube tray.

He had noticed that a duffle bag and two backpacks were stacked at the front door. He asked Mark Halloran where he attended school and what he was studying. "I'm doing graduate work in architecture at the state university, so whatever I can earn I can use for myself and the work of the Lord."

Alster blinked. Margaret came to sit beside her father. He took her hand in his. "Where is the gentleman going to sleep?" he asked.

"Oh, I can bed down anywhere," Mark answered for her. "Margaret has warned me that you would not look favorably . . ."

"I would not!" Alster assured him. "My daughter is only sixteen."

"I could sleep quite comfortably on one of these couches."

Alster looked at the window seat at the green-velvet-upholstered curving steps. At Jane's cushions. "I'm afraid not," he said. "But there is a guest house. For brief visits of company guests. I'll take you down there."

"You're being dreadfully stodgy, Father," said Margaret.

"I always have been, my pet."

"That's funny, because I've bragged of you and Mother as being modern, and Mark and I would consider it a triumph if we could bring Jesus into your lives."

"Jesus has always been in my life," said Alster stiffly. "I was baptised, as you were, when I was an infant. Confirmed, as you were."

"Wait until you see the dear little Episcopal chapel in the woods," said Jane from the kitchen.

"The woods themselves can be our church."

So the evening apparently was going to proceed. Alster took Mark to the guest house and checked him in. Could he help unpack?

"No problem. Books. A razor. I wear sweaters and slacks exclusively." And so he seemed to do, an armful of sweaters, several pairs of slacks. One backpack contained books.

He arranged these things and announced that he would wash his hair back at the house. "I like Maggie's hair dryer."

Alster blinked again. "We've never called her Maggie," he said limply.

"Oh, of course, Margaret is a beautiful name, but her friends— We are pretty informal."

"We are going out to dinner," said Alster, still out of control.

"Good. Then Jane won't have to cook."

Now Alster bit his tongue. They went back to the house, and, sure enough, the young man went upstairs, washed his hair, and came down again with Margaret's blower in his hand. "This way we can visit," he said.

Jane then announced that they were eating out. No, not at the club. There was a crab broiler down the road. . . .

So there was no need to dress. And the crabs were a local feature, though Margaret ordered abalone. "Is it good?"

"It happens to be," said her father.

When they returned home, he said he had rounds to make. Mark offered to go with him.

"You'd be no help," said Alster stiffly.

"I could offer love to the sick, comfort to the dying . . ."

Alster went hurriedly out through the kitchen door. What did that—that *squirt*—know about the sick and certainly about the dying?

"It's the first big thing I have ever known to reach Alster," Jane told Kate Beetz, who called to invite the young people to lunch the next day. Jane said Margaret had walked to the guest house with Mark.

"What's he like?" asked Kate.

"Clean," said Jane, and Kate laughed. So Jane elaborated.

"What about Alster?"

"He's befuddled. Of course, I knew that there never

134

would be a boy child born good enough for his girl."
"You think it's serious?"
"I'm afraid it may be."
"What will you do?"
"What can parents do these days?"
"You sound serious."
"I am serious. But I'll tell you one thing, it has brought Alster and me closer than you would ever have imagined."

The next morning Alster had gone to the hospital at his usual time, with no idea of when the "kids" would arise. Jane was working on her record book, preparing menus for the next thirty days for each group of volunteers. Margaret came downstairs about ten wearing a slinky shift or caftan of pink and white print, her hair tumbled. Had Mark been around, she asked.
"Not that I've seen," said Jane. "Can you fix your own breakfast?"
"I can, but first I want to go out and get some flowers for my hair."
"It needs brushing."
"Oh, Mom . . ."
"One needs to take care of one's hair," said Jane, flipping a page, "and that shift looks pretty revealing, my darling daughter. Remember, we live on a factory complex full of men and windows and stuff."
"You wore a bikini when you swam yesterday afternoon."
"A bikini is an accepted bathing suit. A clinging, thin shift is not."
"Do you want me to change?"
"I think it would be better. So—to quote—go honor thy father and thy mother."
Margaret nodded, and started for the stairs. "I'll call

Mark. How do I do it, and what's for breakfast?"

"Whatever you fix," said Jane firmly.

"Bless you," said Margaret, and went upstairs.

She and Mark had rye crisp and tea for breakfast, swam in the pool, and asked if Alster would be home for lunch.

"He might be able to make it."

"We have something to tell him."

Oh, dear, thought Jane.

Alster said he thought he could get home around noon. "What's for lunch?" he asked.

"I don't think it makes a bit of difference," said Jane.

He did come home a little before twelve. Margaret and Mark were seemingly asleep by the pool.

"What . . . ?" he asked Jane.

"Call the kids inside. I have a salad made, and we'll eat inside."

"Why not?"

"Oh, some foolishness about being shut up between walls."

"In *this* house?" asked Alster, hanging his jacket on the back of a chair.

Jane did not answer him. But he was still looking at the window walls of his home when he went out and told the young people that lunch was about ready. He took the net and scooped some flowers out of the pool.

"They look pretty, Doc," said his daughter.

"They will rot and make a mess. One has to keep a pool clean."

Margaret made an elaborate gesture of raising her eyes to the heavens. "I'll help you," she said, "because I love you so much."

Alster knew that she loved him, but for some reason her manner and her announcement of that love embarrassed him. He kept glancing at the strong-limbed young man, who seemed to be sleeping again. He rapped the sole of his foot with his net pole.

"Lunch!" he said sternly, and went up the steps to the house.

Jane had their salad and their hot rolls ready; she handed Margaret a short robe to put on over her swimsuit, but there was nothing to do about Mark's nudity. He seemed entirely unconcerned that his trunks were skimpy, and Alster did not relish eating at his table with an almost-naked man.

But this was quickly forgotten in things he disliked even more. Because Margaret lost no time in telling her parents that she and Mark were going to be married.

Alster snorted. "You have four years of college before you can even think of it," he said firmly.

Margaret smiled patiently. That smile was getting to her father. "Jesus had no college education; I am sure his mother did not."

"Now see here, Margaret," said her father.

She faced him squarely. "I know everything you want to say," she told him. "But I don't want you to change my mind about this. We are going to be married. We came here to do it with you, and we hoped for your consent."

"You are only sixteen."

"I am sixteen. And I love Mark. We would both rather begin our life together as married."

Wheee!

Alster looked at his wife. "How far can we go along with that?" he asked.

Jane was pale, her face serious. "All the way, I suppose," she said softly. "But, darling—" She turned to Margaret. "You will finish this year of school?"

Margaret shrugged. "I could finish it," she agreed.

"But we are going to be married before break is over."

"How long does that give us?"

"Three weeks. But we could do it today."

No, they could not. Dr. Alster turned to look at Mark Halloran, who was busily cleaning his salad plate. He hated every inch of the young man. The gleam of golden hair on his forearms, the pectoral muscles of his chest . . .

"Tell me about yourself," he said firmly. "If you are going to marry my girl, and I hope make her happy, I would like to know the odds for your doing so. I can guess that you are healthy. Where do you come from? What about your family?"

"Oh, Doc . . ." Margaret protested.

"Let me tell him," said Mark. "I can see his point."

No, he could not, thought Alster. *Oh, God, his—their—dreams for the lovely young girl . . .*

Mark was talking. He came from a small city in Ohio, he said. His father was a civil servant—they were neither rich nor poor. He was a graduate of the state college. He had a degree in architecture.

"And I am a God-fearing Christian," he said. "Margaret loves me for that reason."

"If she knows what it means."

"Let us pray about it," Margaret piped up.

"Hush," said her mother.

Alster nodded. "Do you have a job?" he asked Halloran.

"I can always get one."

"It helps tremendously in any marriage if you have a somewhat common cultural background, as well as food on the table."

"A friendship can be based on the same things."

Yes. It could be. Had they considered the children they might have, he asked.

"We have. I even pointed out to Maggie that at least one of them might look like my uncle who drinks. God will lead us there, too. Now! Shall we pray?"

"For what?" cried Margaret's father in anguish. "Patience with this nonsense?"

"He's angry . . ." murmured Jane.

"I am frightened," cried Alster. "I am scared to death. And I am going back to work!" He rose, slamming his chair hard against the door frame, and stalked out of the house.

He had no idea what Jane said to the young people. He tried to work with concentration. It was as difficult as if he had an aching tooth.

And he did not return to the house until late, to find Margaret in a pretty dress, Mark in a blue ski sweater and blue slacks.

"Good heavens, man!" cried Alster. "It's too warm for a sweater!"

Mark smiled at him. "Margaret has something to tell you," murmured Jane.

"I want a shower before dinner."

"Go ahead. We're eating here."

"No guests?"

"No guests."

He went up the stairs. "Margaret, help your mother," he said.

"Bless you, Father," said Margaret, and Alster swore.

He had always thought of himself as a fairly religious man. But *oh, God! Oh, his dreams for his daughter!*

Jane broke the almost-complete silence of the dinner table. "The children went for a walk this afternoon," she announced, evidently wanting to lift the pall of anger and silence.

Alster said nothing.

Margaret reached out and touched his arm. "We found the most wonderful house," she said.

"Yes?" said her father.

"We pray that it might be our house," she said.

Everyone waited for him to speak. "Where was it? What house?" he asked, sounding as if the words hurt his throat.

Speaking together, the words tumbling, Mark and Margaret told him what house. They had walked up into the woods, they said. "And up and up and *up!*" cried Margaret. "And there was this opening down below us—"

"A beautiful valley," said Mark. "With a small stream—"

"Icy cold, and clear—"

"You don't drink from small streams!" cried her father.

"Oh, Dad. It was too clear—"

"Yes, I know. And Jesus won't let you catch typhoid. Where was the house?"

But he knew. His house. That cube of weathered brown boards, and the aspens, the evergreen trees . . .

"And it is where we are going to live!" cried Margaret, enthusiastically. "Oh, we knew the minute we saw it. The way the sunlight lay on the roof—"

"Which leaks," said Alster.

"Of course it does, darling. But we could fix it up."

"The winters here can be wet, cold, and snowy," said her father.

"But we would have all summer to work on it."

"You're going back to school."

"Oh, I couldn't, now that we've found the house."

His house.

"It belongs to the company," her father pointed out, helping himself to another slice of Jane's good roast.

"But wouldn't they let us? If we patched it up, at our own expense?"

"Who's to provide those expenses?" Alster was feeling better. "You would need furniture, too. Or wouldn't you?"

"We could do without. Sleeping bags and a camp stove." Margaret was getting angry. "We did think you might help us a little."

"Maybe he would, dear," said Jane. "And we do have our furniture in storage."

Alster glared at her. "I think Mark should be planning on a job, rather than taking on a house that is no more than a shack."

"Do you know it?" Jane asked.

"Yes. I take walks, you know. The valley is lovely, the house is not. And it's still company property."

"We could have the water tested."

Yes, they could.

"Would you ask someone . . . ? suggested Mark.

"No, you will have to do that yourself. If you are ready to be responsible for it . . ."

"We would do it no harm."

"A turned-over camp stove could set that whole hillside afire. And while you're at it, why not ask for a job? I do not intend to support you and your family."

"Yes, sir," said Mark.

"Don't pay any attention to him," Margaret told Mark, putting her hand on his arm.

"He'd better pay attention," growled her father. "I don't like any part of this business. This husky fella deciding he can marry a pretty girl and backpack through the rest of his life."

Mark made the mistake of laughing. "That's really good, you know," he told Jane and Margaret.

"Hush," said Jane. "Margaret's father is deeply hurt.

And not the least of that hurt is your threat of taking over his dream home."

The young people stared at Dr. Alster. "Dad . . . ?" said Margaret uncertainly.

Alster got up from the table and walked about. It *was* his dream home, as ridiculous as stating the fact might sound. Margaret was his beloved daughter, also shrouded in dreams—he would have been put to it to voice those dreams in exact terms, but they were there.

"Wouldn't you share your dream house?" Margaret was asking.

"With you kids?"

"Why not? We'd be your family."

Yes, they would be—his family. He sat down again at the table. But he pushed his plate away.

"He's deeply hurt," said Jane, as if he were not present. "And somewhat out of control."

"Alster does not get out of control," said Margaret firmly. Mark was busily eating another slice of roast. How that guy could eat! And did.

But—no. Alster did not get out of control. He drank from his wineglass and smoothed his hand across his cheek. "Where were we?" he asked.

"You were saying that you would not support them," said Jane, her eyes brightly intent.

"And," said Mark, "*I* was about to remark that God would provide."

Alster laughed. "The God I know," he said, "is saying what I do to that. That you are young and healthy—that you cannot lie on your back and read your Bible, with the ravens bringing in prime rib three times a day."

"We don't expect prime rib, or even want that," said Mark.

"Then tell me what it is that you do expect."

"We believe that God will open the way of our lives and show us what we should do."

"While you live in that rundown cabin." Alster leaned across the table. "Don't you know—haven't you learned, Halloran? Margaret has not. Up to now, the ravens have provided for her. But don't *you* know that a man has to get a living some way? He must lie, beg, steal—or even work—for what he needs in life. If he loves a woman, he does these things to feed and protect that woman."

"You don't believe in what you call manna, do you, sir? You have not accepted Jesus."

"What do you know about what I believe in?" cried Alster tightly. He was very angry. "Or what I have accepted? How do you know that your belief is better than mine? I have experience with the results of my ethics and belief. You have not."

Mark evidently heard the anger. "I'll get a job," he told Margaret's father. "I'll work."

"And I'll help him," Margaret piped up.

"Oh, shut up," said Alster. "You're sixteen. The company doesn't hire children."

"She can work in our home," said Mark with dignity. "The Bible—"

Alster put his hand over his ears. "Oh, God," he whispered. "All my dreams!" He paced the room.

"Sir?" said Mark tentatively. Later Alster was to remember every word that was spoken that evening, and he recognized the "sir" as a score for himself. "Sir, what choice of jobs do you think the company could offer me?"

"I don't believe *offer* is the word they would use," said Alster coldly. "But there are jobs you might ask for, and if there are any available . . ."

"What choice of jobs, Alster?" said Jane softly.

Yes. He must stick to the subject.

"Well, let's see. You might be a tracer in the drafting rooms."

"I have a degree in architecture."

"Which may provide advancement for you. But to start—"

"I can train," said Mark, with quiet dignity.

"He really can," said Margaret. "He has whole rolls of yellow paper he calls Bumswat, or something—thin yellow paper—"

"Very cheap," murmured Mark. "It's butter paper, really."

"Er—yes," said Dr. Alster. He sat down in his chair again, but pushed his plate away. The food was cold.

"There's another job usually available," he said gruffly.

Margaret leaned forward. "Tell us, Daddy."

"You haven't called me *Daddy* since you were six."

"Until tonight, you haven't been treating me as if I were six."

He gazed at her, then relaxed. A very little. "I was thinking of a job as sweeper," he said, still gruffly.

Jane's eyebrows went up, but she said nothing.

"I gather that it is not skilled labor," said Mark.

"No, it is not. But when you apply, they may not have the precise job you would want."

"I understand. So tell me about the sweeper job. Is it custodial?"

"No," said Alster, suddenly feeling better. "Sweepers go into an area of the woods where the loggers have been working. They clean up the place."

"And replant trees."

"No. That *is* skilled employment. They just tidy up."

"The complex is a big operation, isn't it?"

"Very big."

"Does a sweeper have a chance for advancement?"

"I suppose any employee has that chance. You would not need your Bumswat in this one."

Mark stood up. "It would, at least, take me out of doors. And that's the life Maggie and I both want, don't we, funny face?"

Jane wished he would not nag at Margaret's father with all the things she knew Alster hated. To call the pretty girl "funny face," to—

"You would have your outdoor life," said Alster. "And funny-face Maggie could wash your dirty clothes in the river. Perhaps she would learn to cook over an open fire, though that is not precisely what we have raised the girl to do."

"Excuse me, Doctor," said Mark, with an excess of dignity, "but I feel that your daughter was a gift of God, and so she grew under His protective care . . ."

"And I didn't raise her at all."

"That's the way we both feel, sir."

Alster got up and left the house. He did wonder what Jane was finding to say to that! She was rather caught in the middle and must find it as difficult as Alster to face, if not accept, the things these young people were heaping upon them.

He was right. When he returned to the house, Jane was waiting for him, her face white and strained.

"I'm sorry . . ." said Alster.

"It's all right, I wanted to walk out, too. Do you want something to eat? You didn't enjoy your dinner . . ."

"Don't set out a meal like that again," he said grimly. *"Prime rib!"*

She made his sandwich and brought a cup of hot coffee with it. "What," she asked, "are we going to *do*, Alster?"

He ate two large bites of meat and bread, drank half the coffee.

"Nothing," he said then.

"But—"

"Time will take care of at least half of our problems."

"But we want them, we want Margaret, to be happy."

"Of course. Just now, she thinks happiness lies in life with Halloran."

"She's too young to know what she wants, what she can be getting into."

"But she is bound to get into it, Jane. If we refuse to let them marry—"

"I know. I know. I don't believe they have been living together, do you?"

"Lord, Jane, I don't know. And maybe it doesn't make any difference."

She stared at him. "I never thought I'd hear you say a thing like that!"

"I never thought I would say it."

"Will he apply for a job?"

"If they mean to live in the canyon house, they will need more than tree bark and camass lilies. Yes, he will apply. And then he will come to me, or Joe, for a physical examination. I only hope he doesn't try again to tell me that I didn't raise the girl he wants to marry."

"Won't Margaret have to have an examination, too?"

"If they marry, and he's company employed, yes, she will."

"And it's my turn to ask—or hope—that she won't say all the wrong things."

"I believe they have all been said."

"Probably. This job—is it a good one?"

"What is a good job? The one of sweeper is hard

work, but good pay. He'll probably take it on that basis."

"Well, at least we shall have Margaret close."

"I am alarmed about that."

She turned her head to look directly at him. "What do you mean, *alarmed*?"

"You've never been up to the canyon and the house, have you? Well, the canyon, and the house—they are about as primitive as one can get and still hear airplanes flying over. To think of Margaret staying in that house alone, especially at night—"

"Will she?"

"The crews go where the work is. Halloran will be with the crew. She cannot go with him. They want to live in the canyon. It adds up, Jane, my sweet, to our daughter living alone in a house without so much as a decent door, let alone a lock."

"Then they can't live there."

"We have tried to say they cannot be married."

"Would you let her . . . she can come back here if Mark has to be away."

"No, sir! If she marries him, she lives the life he provides for her."

"You don't mean that."

"I hope I do."

"But—if it's dangerous . . ."

"I don't know how dangerous it is, Jane. That pretty canyon is several miles back into the woods. There's a logging road, grown over. Margaret could be safe in the house one night, one week maybe, a month, even for a year. Then—of course, if God really is taking care of her . . . I'd set myself up to be his deputy."

"And there is danger."

"From animals, you mean."

"Yes. I mean all sorts of animals. Chipmunks." Jane

smiled. "Bobcats," said Alster. "Bears—and men."
Jane stared at him. "You're serious?" she asked breathlessly.
"Of course I am serious. Fugitive men, backpacking hikers, hunters—men. That house affords shelter. No one expects people to be living there."
"Then we cannot allow . . "
"Jane, you have heard me talk to these young people. I don't expect Margaret to be realistic, though I did hope she was intelligent. Mark is enough older—"
"He's a kook, a freak. If he works, and earns even a tiny salary, they could have a safer place to live—"
"But don't you see? He—and she—*want* to live in the woods, among all the primitive things that were found in Eden. Flowers, trees, wild animals—and men. I have said I would not support them. Mark is capable of doing that himself. But he chooses to ignore the progress that the world has made. He is still, he claims, a follower of Jesus on the shore of Galilee. And I suppose it is going to fall to me to protect my daughter."
"Which we would do."
"Yes. Which I will do."
"This whole thing is wrong, Alster."
"Yes, of course it is. And that wrong terrifies me. Because, in a year or so, my daughter, still a child, will have to acknowledge that I am right."
"But she will stick with it."
"And *that* is what terrifies me. Her whole life . . ." He sat and stared before him. "Since she was born," he said, "I have faced the time when some man would come wanting to marry my daughter. And I have actually prayed that it would be a man of the same culture and taste that we were giving her."
Jane took her knitting out of its basket. "You didn't

give any thought to the physical appeal of the wrong man?"

"I did. But I prayed that both circumstances would prevail."

"This may work out, you know," said Jane quietly.

"If she would just agree to finish school . . ."

"She will finish, some day." Jane changed needles.

Alster glanced at her. "I don't see," he said, "how you can be so calm."

"I am not calm at all. But you are upset enough, and showing enough, for two of us."

"She'll learn . . ."

"And so will we."

"Yes, we will. Where are they this evening?"

"Oh, they've gone up the green slopes of the forest, with the purple mountains rising behind them."

Alster made a profane sound and said he was going to bed.

The next day Joe Raithel met Margaret Alster.

And without knowing who she was, he immediately fell head over heels in love with her. He was stunned. He had thought this day, and the ones following it, would be unbearably difficult, what with Charles's death, and Dr. Alster's insistence that he return at once to work. And it had begun so. He was tired, he was drained of all interest in patients or hospital routine.

And then he saw Margaret. The prettiest girl he had ever seen! Smiling, walking with grace and assurance, her dark blond hair bobbing against the shoulders of her white blouse, her pretty legs and the swirl of her dark-blue skirt—and her smile! She smiled at Joe when she passed him and said, "Hi!"—without knowing who he was. Just as he didn't know who she was. He hoped that she was a new employee, or at least wanted to be one. He watched her go toward the business offices.

He would hang around and see if she came out before he actually had to go back into the hospital. Maybe they could eat lunch together, and listen to the music, and talk—

Margaret's purpose was the simplest. She herself would go straight to Mr. Pemscot and ask if she and Mark could live in the canyon house. If Mark secured a job, she could take care of where they would live.

Mr. Pemscot was not in his office, but probably would be later that day. And when she came out into the corridor again, there was that solemn-faced young man, a doctor by his clothing, ready to ask if he could be of help.

Margaret smiled at him and said, "Why, yes, you could. Maybe." Was he a doctor? Yes, he was Joe Raithel.

"And you work with my father . . ."

"Dr. Alster is your father?"

Later, talking to Jane, talking lyrically about his encounter with Margaret, he told her all this, even about his surprise that Dr. Alster should have such a daughter.

Jane had laughed at him. "But why? With me for her mother?"

This had thrown him into a tizzy of apology and explanation. The best he could do was to say that he would have considered Jane too young . . .

But he had been smitten with the girl. Yes, they could eat lunch in the courtyard. Margaret wasn't hungry, but she would talk to him and listen to the music. And this they did. They talked endlessly. Margaret knew that Mark could find her there on the grounds—if he needed to find her.

And this young doctor had so much to say—about her, about her father—even about Jane. He told about the graffitis and Margaret laughed merrily. Her mother had certainly not told her about that!

"I thought it was terrible at the time," said Joe solemnly, "but I could share a thing like that with a girl like you, Margaret."

"Be fun," she agreed.

"I'd be proud. I suppose—no, I *know*—I've been waiting for you, for a girl like you, all my life."

"I think he really meant it," Margaret later told Jane, who was not so amused at the way their talk had gone. She was closer to Doc's age than was Margaret.

"Did you tell him about your plan to marry Mark and live in a placer miner's shack?" asked her mother coolly.

"Oh, I had to tell him that I was going to be married."

"And—"

"Well, he was jealous. Insanely jealous, Mom. He talked almost worse than Dad. All about another man touching me—stuff like that."

"Didn't he have work to do in the hospital? And where on earth was Mark all the time this love at first sight was going on?"

"Oh, I learned later that he had ridden up to one of the logging sites and he—Joe, I mean—was called away. To do his hospital doctoring, I suppose. He had a beeper thing in his coat pocket, and he left. I just sunbathed on the grass, and he came back."

"You must have given the employees something to talk about."

"We didn't do a thing but sit and talk, Mom. And

finally he was so excited and upset he told me about his brother—"

"Yes, he died last week. Doc was very fond of him."

"And he told me how he had tried to save his life, that of his own accord he had used medicine that was not usually prescribed, but which he had hoped—I think that was a very brave thing."

Foolhardy, Jane told herself. Unethical. And definitely dangerous.

"Did he say what the medicine was?" she asked aloud, her tone and manner cool.

"Oh, I don't know about those things. Yes, he did say. Chlore—something or other."

Jane nodded. She knew.

"Joe called it a bold move," said Margaret.

"Mmmm," murmured Jane, pretending not to be interested. "What's happened to Mark?"

"Oh, he'll be here soon. He said he would need a shower before dinner."

"Why don't you two go out somewhere for dinner?" Jane suggested. "You must have a lot to talk about."

Margaret laughed. "But we don't have a lot of money. Could we sign Dad's name at the club?"

"You would have to ask him."

"And he'll say no. I *wish* he liked Mark, Mom."

"He wouldn't like any man you'd plan to marry, as young as you are."

"Oh," cried Margaret. "That's *nowhere!*"

"So is dinner," said Jane. "Look, I'll give you five dollars and you go down the road to a hamburger place. Your Mark will really enjoy that. And your father can have something like a peaceful evening. I forgot to ask. Did you ever see Mr. Pemscot?"

"No. Joe talked so long—"

He must have. To Margaret. To others. Alster came

"You'll stay within two feet of me until she leaves. What do you suppose she wants?"

"Joe's told her . . ."

But Alster was opening the door and greeting their caller, who was, at the least, agitated.

Yes, she said, something *was* wrong. Yes, something *had* happened. She looked around, and up the stairs, and asked how they had ever got the piano up there, and what did the Alsters think of Joe's behavior?

Alster urged her to sit down, and asked what behavior she had in mind. "I think Joe has had a difficult week," murmured Jane.

"Oh, he has, he has. He takes things so hard. And he is so young. You really should not have asked him to come back so soon."

Alster blinked. "I felt he was needed."

"Yes, but he was so upset, so despondent that he had not been able to help Charles, and I am sure he was just hysterical when he said all that about being in love with your daughter and marrying her, and not letting anything prevent. Where is she? I would like to see her, at least."

"She has gone out for dinner, Mrs. Raithel. And I am sure you misunderstood Joe."

"Oh, no, I didn't. He was like—well, I don't know—he walked around and clapped his hands and said that he had hoped to find a girl this way, just out of the blue, and he could not believe his luck. I confess, Mrs. Alster—Doctor—that I was shocked. His behavior, and the way he talked. Men just don't come across a girl in a hospital corridor and decide they are going to marry her. Though I am sure your daughter would be very nice."

"She is nice," Jane agreed. "She is home on spring

in asking what on earth the kids had been up to that day. Where were they, by the way?

Jane told him about the hamburgers, and he laughed. He gave her the five dollars and mixed drinks for them both. "Do we eat?" he asked.

"Oh, yes. I have the crockpot full."

"Wouldn't there have been enough . . . ?"

"Don't you need a quiet evening? And I'll get my records up to date."

"Good girl. Joe Raithel is back."

"I know." But she said no more. Then.

"We're going to have to do more than eat chicken stew and lemon sherbet," he reminded his wife.

"Yes. I know."

"What happened today?"

"Nothing, really. But I'll talk about it later."

"Well, I guess something did happen, because Joe Raithel asked me what my answer would be if he asked to marry my daughter."

Jane laughed. And Alster stared at her.

"What did you say?"

"I told him that bigamy was illegal at sixteen."

Jane nodded. "As good an answer as you could have found," she told him.

They lingered over dinner. It was after eight o'clock when Jane decided to put things away in the kitchen, and she was busy at the task when Alster heard her say, "Oh, oh!"

He set his book aside. "Now what?" he asked. "Not Murphy?"

"No. I haven't seen Murphy in days. It's Mrs. Raithel."

"Can I escape?"

"You know you can't. So put on your charm and let her in. I'll finish up here."

153

"You'll stay within two feet of me until she leaves. What do you suppose she wants?"

"Joe's told her . . ."

But Alster was opening the door and greeting their caller, who was, at the least, agitated.

Yes, she said, something *was* wrong. Yes, something *had* happened. She looked around, and up the stairs, and asked how they had ever got the piano up there, and what did the Alsters think of Joe's behavior?

Alster urged her to sit down, and asked what behavior she had in mind. "I think Joe has had a difficult week," murmured Jane.

"Oh, he has, he has. He takes things so hard. And he is so young. You really should not have asked him to come back so soon."

Alster blinked. "I felt he was needed."

"Yes, but he was so upset, so despondent that he had not been able to help Charles, and I am sure he was just hysterical when he said all that about being in love with your daughter and marrying her, and not letting anything prevent. Where is she? I would like to see her, at least."

"She has gone out for dinner, Mrs. Raithel. And I am sure you misunderstood Joe."

"Oh, no, I didn't. He was like—well, I don't know—he walked around and clapped his hands and said that he had hoped to find a girl this way, just out of the blue, and he could not believe his luck. I confess, Mrs. Alster—Doctor—that I was shocked. His behavior, and the way he talked. Men just don't come across a girl in a hospital corridor and decide they are going to marry her. Though I am sure your daughter would be very nice."

"She is nice," Jane agreed. "She is home on spring

vacation, and she is pretty. But I think you exaggerate . . ."

"No, I do not," said Mrs. Raithel firmly.

"Then I would suggest that Joe did," said Dr. Alster.

"But," said the poor woman, "as excited as he was—is. Young people do foolish things. He is in no position just now to be married."

"Then he can't be in any danger of getting married," said Alster dryly.

Mrs. Raithel turned on him. "But the way he *talked*, Doctor! And a girl as excited as he is—"

"Is she?" asked Jane. "As excited?"

"Well, you know his appeal to women, Mrs. Alster."

Jane took a step back. "I think," she said coldly, "that all you have to base your fears on, Mrs. Raithel, is the excited talk of a young man who thinks he has fallen in love. Yes, I know he talked. Young people do talk under those circumstances. They talk wildly, but it's all foam, my dear woman, foam on the beer."

She thought her metaphor would stop Mrs. Raithel, and it did. She gasped and fished in her purse for a Kleenex. "I am so upset," she said, as if to herself. Alster looked reprovingly at his wife, who shrugged and went to sit on the window seat until this woman got control of herself.

It took a little time, and Alster became somewhat exasperated. Finally he said firmly that Mrs. Raithel surely knew that she could not live her son's life, nor direct the way he lived it.

Mrs. Raithel looked up at him, first in affront, then with anxiety. "But you must know, Dr. Alster, that my son is an especially fine doctor . . ."

Quickly Jane looked at her husband; his face was impassive. Waiting. "It would be a fine thing," Mrs. Raithel continued, "if he would marry the right girl.

But your daughter, I understand, is only sixteen; she is too young, she needs to go to school."

"And you came here to tell me to stop this marriage."

"I am sure he would listen to you and your advice."

"Only if it meant his job. Parents," he said grimly, "come pretty low on the totem pole."

"I don't understand," said poor Mrs. Raithel.

Jane came to her rescue. "We all like Doc," she said warmly. "Perhaps it is hard on you that you live together. You are seeing him go through what most young doctors do. Learning, and stumbling—"

Mrs. Raithel straightened. "My son," she said, with enormous dignity, "is brilliant. In school—working with Dr. Anderson—and now. Have you forgotten the way he studied and learned about the use of chloromycetin for his brother's leukemia, and kept him alive?"

"Your son had aplastic anemia," said Jane. Alster had walked to the front door.

"Joe," said Mrs. Raithel, still dignified, "called Charles's illness leukemia."

Jane's eyebrows went up. "Go on," she said.

"And he gave the medication to Charles."

"He did, indeed," said Jane, wishing, but not expecting, that Alster would join this little skirmish.

But he said nothing. Nothing at all. He let the woman go on and on about the brilliance of her son; she talked until Margaret came into the house from the poolside and overheard some of what she said. Jane saw her and hoped she could get Joe's mother out and away before she need meet Margaret.

She succeeded by moving steadily toward Mrs. Raithel, seeming to listen to her talk, and with her hand on her shoulder, guiding her out through the front door and to her car. "You're still too much affected by the death of your son," she said kindly, "to be concerned about anything except getting your nerves settled." These women loved to be told that they *had* nerves.

She came back into the house, fanning her face with her hands.

"What was all that about?" Margaret asked.

"She was worried lest you decide to marry her brilliant son and ruin his career."

Margaret peeled a banana and bit off the end of it. "Is he so brilliant?" she asked.

"He does very well, but he's hardly the genius his mother thinks he is. Did you have a good dinner?"

"Mark ate five hamburgers."

"He'll never in the world earn enough to feed himself," said Alster. "I'm going to bed."

The next day, Margaret came downstairs at an unusually early hour. She wanted breakfast, she said.

"Mark ate the whole five dollars worth of hamburgers?" Jane asked. She was busy at the small round table, papers and a book or two spread out; she was writing busily on a pad of legal-size paper.

"What's for breakfast?" asked Margaret.

"Anything you want," said Jane, writing busily.

"What are you doing?"

"You know I free-lance articles for the newspaper," said her mother.

"Can't you stop and feed your child?" asked that child.

Jane glanced at her. "If you can't fix your own breakfast, how on earth . . . ?"

"OK, OK," said Margaret hastily. "I'll do it. But what I really want to do is to talk about the wedding." She brought out a box of cereal, she checked on the coffeemaker. She found cream and a small can of pineapple juice. "Will there be a little place for me on your table?" she asked.

Jane stacked some of the papers. "But don't splash," she suggested.

"Mother . . ."

"Mmmm?"

"I suppose you and Dad have decided to ignore the fact that Mark and I plan to be married."

"Was that Mark's idea?"

"He thinks it could be the method you hope to use."

"We haven't given it a serious thought," Jane agreed.

"Well, you had better."

"Don't drink out of the can, dear."

Margaret fetched a glass, filled it with juice, poured cereal into a large bowl, added cream and sugar, found a spoon, filled a coffee mug. "We made all our plans last night," she said quietly.

"That's good," said Jane. "because I am busy—"

"Mother!"

"I'm listening." Jane reached for one of the thick books.

"That's a medical book," said Margaret.

"I am writing an article on a medical subject."

"Why don't you let Dad do that?"

"He doesn't write newspaper articles."

"I suppose he could. Well, anyway—there is a man coming. Can he stay at the guest house?"

"What man is it? And when does all this happen?"

"Next week. Whenever Billy Bob can get here. Mark's calling him this morning."

"Next week—hmmm. Yes, I'll be free then. Meanwhile you and Mark should talk to the rector . . ."

Margaret stood up and leaned across the table.

"Mother!" she said loudly. "Will you *listen* to me?"

Jane dropped her pencil and leaned back in her chair. She was wearing white Bermuda shorts, a red sweatshirt, and her hair was twisted into a shining knot. "I am listening," she said patiently. "But I do want to get this article written. And I have to pack for a short trip with Alster. Do you want to come along? We'll be back Tuesday. You'll love San Francisco. We—"

"Hold it," said Margaret. She sat down and began to eat the cereal rapidly. "Just hold it," she said. "And then you really listen to me. Because I am saying to you that Mark and I are going to be married. We really are."

"When?" asked Jane. "You have already used up the first week of your three-week break."

"I am not home on 'break,' Mother dear," said Margaret patiently. "I am not going back to school. I am going to be married. And soon. Very soon. As soon as we hear from Billy Bob."

"Whoever that is. But it makes no difference, because a wedding means plans to make."

"What plans?" asked Margaret coldly. "A white dress, I suppose, and flowers, and a church organ? Engraved invitations and pink champagne?"

"Your father would never allow pink champagne at your wedding. But he certainly would want things done, if at all, in the manner customary to our class and position in life."

Margaret stared at her. "After all we have said to you, you still would mention *class* to me?" she demanded.

"Why not? You belong to a certain class—or culture, if you like the word better."

"I don't like it one bit better. You've met Mark,

you've talked to him. I love him—"

"Physically, he's a fine specimen. But do you know anything about his family? Are they coming to this wedding that you are planning?"

"Everyone who loves me will be there," said Margaret.

"You say that you have made plans?"

"Oh, that we will go through the necessary things. License, blood tests, an authorized person to witness the ceremony."

"And there is to be a ceremony?"

"Maybe not in the sense you mean. Candles, a needlepoint wedding kneeler. But then, you would look awful in pale blue chiffon, Mother. You really would."

"Where will you have this wedding?"

"Up the mountain, with the sky above us and the trees whispering the processional."

"Margaret, will you please stop this? I really should make a recording to play back to you six weeks from now, to show you how nauseating you sound."

"You asked about our plans. I've told you."

"Then your father and I can take this trip we have planned for next week. Will you go with us? We hoped you would."

"I don't think so. We could perhaps have the wedding before you go."

"We leave day after tomorrow. Did Mark get a job?"

"Of a sort. And someone called Pigeon is going to help us make the house livable."

Jane nodded. "Margaret, you are getting into something that you know nothing—absolutely *nothing*—about!"

"Yes, and I rejoice."

"You do? The cold, the isolation?"

"If we can't take it, we can always rent a three-room apartment with a microwave oven."

Jane laughed. "Three-room apartments don't come so equipped. And you had better ask your father about the pill."

"He brought the subject up and we told him that we were letting God decide when we would have children."

"And what did Alster say?"

"Oh, you know what he said. That we could expect the first one nine months and ten minutes after the wedding."

Jane laughed, not amused at all. "You are hurting us both," she said. "You know that."

"But I feel that it's your fault, not ours. When do you leave for San Francisco?"

"I shan't go at all, and leave you here alone."

"Oh, *Mother!*"

"Now, look. You claim your right to do things your way. Don't I have the same privilege?"

Margaret looked sulky. "Talk about playing back a record," she muttered. "But all right. Do you know where to find a baby-sitter?"

"If I can't—"

"You won't go, and that will put Dad into a bigger tizzy than he is already."

"It certainly will. For this morning, have you made your bed and tidied your room?"

"What about Mrs. Beetz?"

"No."

"I like her."

"So do I. But she wouldn't do this. Though maybe Hilda Curren would—"

Margaret groaned. "She would be worse than you are."

"That's why I shall ask her. And I think Michael should be asked to conduct the ceremony."

"He would want it to be in the church."

"Yes, he would."
"Billy Bob would be better."
"Is he . . . ?"
"He's a preacher. It was through him that Mark and I met. He understands young people."

Her mother made no comment and Margaret went upstairs.

That evening Jane told Alster of the conversation. "Did you call Mike?"

"Yes, I did . . ."

"And?"

"He says if we don't go along with this, we may lose our child."

"Margaret knows that. She knows she can threaten us."

"Won't we have to sign a permission?"

"Yes. One of us will have to. Is Hilda going to stay here?"

"She understands the spot we're in."

"Yes. But I feel sorry for her."

Jane and Alster returned from the three-day medical meeting to find the wedding imminent, and their house full of strange people.

"They are called 'Saints,'" said Hilda, herself as near tears as ever they were to see that sturdy soul. "I think this was all planned before Margaret ever left Ohio, because these young people— Why, there are even wedding gifts!"

Shocked, Jane and Alster looked at the items spread out upon a table. A clothes basket filled with health foods, a tie-dye tablecloth. The doctor picked up a small flat box. "This is a crucifix!" he pointed out to Margaret.

"I know. Isn't it beautiful?"

"It's Roman Catholic!"

"Dad . . ."

"All right. Tell me what is going to happen. Every damned thing!"

"It will be beautiful."

"Tell me."

So she told him. So it happened.

The first thing he did was to clear the "guests" out of the house and assure Hilda that he and Jane were forever in her debt.

"All I did," said that sturdy soul, "was to see that Margaret slept in the room with me every night."

"Well, now I want them out. I find bare feet revolting; long, stringy hair, chains— Saints, indeed!" He gave his orders. Bedrolls, banjos, and guitars—all were to get off of company property. What must the company think? And the town?

Everybody, said Margaret, was thrilled. They had been invited—

"Did Pigeon— What about the house?"

"Well, he said we couldn't live in it where it was. That the fire protection machinery couldn't get to it. So the men have been cutting it and moving it to the riverside, just off of company land, up the mountain and across the river."

"Wait a minute, wait a minute! How did they cut it?"

"In four pieces, then put it together again. It's really stronger and better now. And they put in windows and doors. It's really lovely, Dad."

Alster mopped his brow.

"But you'll see it on Sunday," Margaret promised. "After the ceremony and the feast we all will walk up the mountainside to our home."

"Can you believe this?" Alster asked Jane.

"I am more concerned in getting a crew in here to

clean our house. I suspect fleas, if no worse."

Hilda touched her arm. "Wait a minute," she said. "These kids—they may not be the 'Saints' they call themselves, but they were here this evening to welcome you. They did not stay here while you were gone. They have a bus and a motor home, which they drove from Ohio. They are preparing for the wedding, yes, and it won't be like anything you would plan. But these past three days—Mark found some land on the far side of the river where he could set up the house."

"Cut into four pieces," said Alster dryly.

"Yes, they did that. They have got some furniture through Goodwill. The women, the girls, have planted a garden. They have their bus and camper parked up there. The wedding will be on the hill overlooking Alster's canyon, and the young folk have made the arrangements. I talked to Murphy, and he said to let them alone. They did not stay here while you were away. In the evenings they would come here, yes, bare feet and stringy hair, and I am sure, tired muscles. They would sit in a circle out by the pool, play their guitars, sing hymns, talk—and touch each other."

"One of them called me *Mamma,*" said Jane, her tone bewildered, though she tried to laugh. "Alster, I feel like putting Margaret into the car and running off."

"She wouldn't go," said Hilda.

"When is the wedding?" Alster asked.

"Sunday, at sunrise. You don't have to provide food; the Saints will bring some."

"I'll bet. Sunrise, eh? That comes pretty early."

"Have you met Billy Bob?"

"If he's the fat, bearded one, I have. And if it takes him to get me into heaven . . ."

"What about Margaret's clothes?" asked Jane.

"That, too, is arranged. You just be there. Please?"

"On Sunday morning," said Jane, swallowing the sob in her throat.

"Is Murphy coming?" asked Alster.

"I sincerely hope not."

But he was there. And the rain that Alster had asked for did not materialize. But the wedding did take place. "I didn't think it would," said most of the Friday-nighters.

"What do we wear?" asked Alster, very early that Sunday morning. "I've never been in this situation before. Is it all right if I shave?"

Jane did not answer him. "I'll ask Margaret," she said.

But Margaret was not in her room, though her bed had been slept in.

Jane came back to tell her husband. "Maybe we shouldn't go?"

"That's the easy way out. What will you wear?"

"Anything but pale blue chiffon," said Jane, brushing her hair.

They settled on light suits. Drank a cup of coffee, locked the house, and started out, to find themselves a part of a procession making its way up the mountainside.

"Our loyal friends," murmured Jane.

"And our curious ones."

"They attend every wedding. As for myself, if this were happening to someone else, I'd laugh."

"It's usual for the mother of the bride to cry," said Alster, taking her arm. "Did you wear sensible shoes?"

"The only sensible thing on this damn mountain."

But as many as fifty people made the trek. "We look like a line of ants going to a picnic," growled Alster.

And when they reached the top, there was Billy Bob, in vestments, to Jane's outraged surprise. Murphy Anderson laughed at her. "You wanted a formal wedding," he reminded her.

But not that young, fat, bearded . . .

There were guitars, and Mark in what someone told them was a Mexican wedding shirt—loose, embroidered, his chest well exposed.

And the sun came up— What were they waiting for?

"The girls have made an arch of flowers. They must have overslept."

Even Margaret appeared, in a gleaming dress of gold matelassé.

"My caftan!" breathed Jane. She looked accusingly at Hilda.

"You would gladly have given her white satin and Alençon lace."

Yes, Jane would have. "Why don't we start?"

"Why," asked some bright soul, "don't we have the reception first and the wedding afterward? The ice is melting in the punch."

It was not real. It simply was not real! But they drank the fruit juice and ate the little cakes of oats and rice.

And Jane gazed at her daughter. Never more lovely, a wreath of yellow jonquils in her hair.

And, finally, here came the six girls with the flowery arch. They had made the framework the night before, put the flowers on at four that morning, and then could not get the edifice out through the door of the bus. It had had to be—well, anyway, here they were, and the ceremony could proceed.

"Are you giving her away?" Jane whispered to Alster.

"If asked. Listen."

Billy Bob was explaining the flowers in the ceremony. Margaret carried a blue rose. The bridesmaids each carried a single rose, a red one for passion, a yellow for wisdom, a white for purity . . . There was some singing, and a good deal of talking back and forth between bride and groom, between each of them and the priest, between the priest and the congregation, which, tired from the climb, was sitting on rocks, or flat on the ground. Afterward, Alster helped Jane to her feet, and they, with Murphy Anderson, started down the trail. Jane paused and stood gazing down into what she called Alster's canyon. "It's pretty," she said. The aspens were in new leaf, the evergreens dark against the silvery shale of the placer diggings. And the square spot of bare ground . . .

"My house is gone," said Alster.

"Can't you manage one to take its place?"

He appeared to be considering the idea.

"I think the company might let you," said Murphy. "Maybe one of those ready-cut A-frame things."

"I'll see," said Alster, his shoulders straightening.

"It's strange," he said. "This wedding today. I know the prayer book service so well. This preacher fella—and was he ever folksy?—all I can quote was what he said to those kids by way of instruction. Let's see. He said that 'God has a plan and purpose for your life. You know that part of that plan was for you to find Jesus as your Savior, to get married, and to raise a family.' "

He walked another ten feet. "Do you think they are married, Murph?"

"As married as they need to be. But the fellow sure isn't any Cranmer."

"And I have one thing to be thankful for," said Alster. "She didn't marry Raithel."

"Was there a chance of that?" asked Dr. Anderson, surprised.

"His mother thought there was," Jane told him.

"Well!"

"Don't you like Joe?" Jane asked her husband.

"He's a ninny."

"Oh—"

"Of course, he will probably make all sorts of money as a doctor, with that earnest manner of his."

Murphy grinned at Jane, but she was thinking of other things. "I wish," she said, "that we had followed the kids, and gone with them to see their home."

"You can see it at any time," said Murphy.

"If invited," Alster amended, his tone cool.

"And," said Jane, "they will show up regularly at our house. Especially at mealtime."

"If invited," said Alster again.

Jane pulled free from his helping hand. "There must have been a better way to handle that whole getting-married thing," she said crossly. "And I don't mean Joe Raithel. Though *ninny* is not what I would call him."

Murphy and Alster exchanged interested glances. She knew Raithel better than they did. But Jane had said all she meant to say. She twirled the blue rose in her hand and strode down the path. She wished she had refused to accept the thing from Margaret. "I am going to show them," she whispered to herself.

"What them?" asked Alster.

But Jane did not answer him. She was angry, and the men could only guess why. They came upon five of the Saints asleep in the shade of a clump of young evergreens. "It can't be booze," said Alster.

"No, but I am going to claim the champagne you owe me."

"No wedding," said Alster, "no champagne. But for

some reason, I could join that unsavory crew. I am tired!"

"We'll make it stronger than champagne," said Murphy. "It's not nine o'clock, and already this has been a long, hard day."

7

It was a week later that Jane brought a handful of fluttering proof sheets to Alster where he lounged beside the pool. Having had a good swim, he now was stretched out in a long chair.

"You'll get suntanned in spots," Jane warned him, looking up at the blowing trees. "Do you want to read this?"

"What is it?"

"Proofs of an article I wrote."

"Sell it?"

"It's to run in the Baumgarten newspaper."

"For free." He put the papers on the low table and weighted them with a book. "I'll read it later."

"Better do it now. You won't be happy."

His eyes brightened. "What have you done now that you shouldn't?" he asked.

"The Baumgarten editor called it a bombshell. He said it was well researched and well written."

"And it's a bombshell."

"Read it and see."

Alster groaned and straightened in the chair, pulling up against the back. He took the strips of paper. He read the first paragraph and glanced at Jane. She had slipped off her covering robe and gone into the pool. "I would have invited the kids to dinner," she said, "but we haven't arranged smoke signals."

"You can always reach Mark through the complex. Leave a message, that is."

"Now why didn't I think of that? Margaret's school things came this week. I had the boxes put up in her room."

"Clothes, I suppose."

"Clothes and books, tennis rackets and skis. She'll find so many of the things useful. Especially the bikinis and the formal prom dresses. Maybe they'll have a garage sale."

"Can't. No garage. Look, Jane you can't publish this thing."

"Why not? It's like the man said, well researched."

"But—the editor's right. It is a bombshell."

He read "the thing" again, half aloud. Jane lay on a floating plastic cushion and watched him. She had really drawn blood.

"There isn't a person over there who won't identify this death," he said.

"I make no charges. I name no one."

"Oh, no, you don't. You just say that—has Raithel seen this?"

"No. Of course not."

"Well, get him down here. *Stat!*"

Jane slipped off the cushion and came to the edge of the pool, shaking water from her face. "You gave up your right to *stat* orders when you married me, Dr. Alster," she said coldly.

He groaned. "That's only one thing I did," he assured her. He got up and went into the house. She could see him using the telephone. And she lay down again on the long blue and white cushion. She was paying off a handful of scores, and she knew that she looked beautiful doing it. She had the figure of a twenty-year-old woman. Alster might not appreciate that, but other men did.

He came back.

"Did you call Murphy?" asked Jane.

"Hasn't he seen this thing? Really, Jane—"

"It's interesting, and it is factual. And I did not—"

"You did not like Joe Raithel's falling flat on his face over Margaret. And you need very badly to get back at Joe's mother."

"Oh, Alster. I just saw an interesting story—"

"Mmmm. And all you say is that a case affecting well-known local people has added to the increasing evidence that a widely used antibiotic sometimes may kill rather than cure."

Yes, that was the way she had begun it.

Joe Raithel was coming down the sloping lawn. "Is something wrong, Dr. Alster?" he asked, while still ten feet away. "Hello, Jane."

She flipped her hand and smiled.

"I had something to show you, and talk over with you," said Alster. "I thought, what with beepers, you'd rather discuss it here."

"Yes, sir?"

The young man sat down. Jane nodded. Yes, he might be considered a ninny.

Fresh-faced, innocent-eyed. And yes, he would get rich. He always wanted to please. Right now, he was trying that with Alster.

"I never examined your brother Charles," said Alster, "nor was I asked to. And I agree with this article that no single piece of evidence, up to now—and there has been a series of studies—no definite link has been established between the drug chloramphenicol and aplastic anemia."

As he was speaking, color began to rise in Dr. Raithel's cheeks. "My brother died of leukemia," he said stiffly. "I never accepted the diagnosis of aplastic anemia."

"That doesn't mean he did not have it. And the chances of its development among persons taking this drug are very small. This article says that."

"May I see the article, sir?"

"I'll let you read it. Yes. The point is, there have been warnings both from the FDA and the American Medical Society against the use of the drug. Thirty years ago there was an attempt to restrict or even ban its use. And we still get warnings against the potential toxicity of the drug."

"But, sir, it is effective against a great many illnesses."

Alster's eyebrows went up. "Did your brother have his own physician—of course he did!"

"Yes, sir, but the antibiotics used had most unpleasant side effects."

"They often do. Would you give chloramphenicol in a case of minor illness?"

"No, sir."

Dr. Alster folded the proof sheets neatly, but continued to hold them in his hand. "Perhaps you prescribed chloromycetin?"

"No, sir—" His attention centered. "Where did you get the idea that I had done so?"

"Your mother told us that you had done so."

"Oh . . ."

"And she brought us a bag full of medicines that he had been taking."

This threw the young doctor into a panic. He got up from his chair and paced the area surrounding the pool. Alster sat quietly and watched him. Jane got out of the water, wrapped her hair into a turban with a towel, put on her cover-up robe.

"My mother," the young man stammered. "I am sure she did not mean to hurt me."

"I doubt if she has," said Alster quietly.

"But if that article says, or even implies, that I hastened Charles's death. Who wrote it, Dr. Alster? You surely didn't."

"I wouldn't bother. But I certainly don't want you experimenting with any of my patients."

"I was trying desperately to help Charles."

"Who was beyond help."

"Yes, maybe he was. Anyway— Oh, I *wish* Mother had kept out of this."

"I don't think she has any idea that you harmed your brother."

"She will have that idea if she gets hold of that article. And the way she talks— May I read it, sir?"

Alster extended the folded papers. Dr. Raithel took them and walked away to stand against a flowering hedge and read them. Dr. Alster stretched out in his chair. Jane would have gone into the house, but Alster detained her. "Stick it out," he said firmly.

"Did you write this?" Dr. Raithel asked, his eyes still on the papers.

"Not me," said Dr. Alster.

Joe looked across the pool to Jane. "I always thought you liked me," he said accusingly.

"She always thought that *you* liked *her*," drawled Alster.

"I do." He was frowning. "I do. But, of course—"

"I shouldn't advise you to say it," said Alster quickly.

"Can this be published?" asked Joe.

Alster shrugged. "She has her facts straight. Any confusion in terms originated with you. If you did give your brother chloramphenicol and withdrew or opposed the attending physician's prescribed medication—"

"My mother meant well when she brought you the medicines, though she should have given them to me."

"There are a lot of 'should haves' in this whole situation, Doctor."

"I—"

"You were acting as a brother, not a doctor. But you will have to learn, young man, that that is a no-no in our profession. We simply cannot let our personal interests rule what we do. The sick man under your hand at any given moment has a claim on you over your child, your wife, or your—"

"Do you think I cannot fill that obligation?"

"I think you did *not* fill it where your brother was concerned."

"No. I suppose not. But when I saw the chloramphenicol was a mistake, I did try to correct it."

"And Charles would have died anyway."

"Yes. Yes, he would. And, of course, this means the end of medicine for me."

"Oh, don't be so damn young, Joe!" In one swift surge, Alster was up and out of his chair.

"If she publishes this—"

"Those are proof sheets," said Jane. "The article will be published."

"I don't suppose it makes any difference. I can't be fired from a position I no longer hold, nor keep a professional rank I am ready to surrender."

Alster said something below his breath, and Jane giggled.

Dr. Raithel was still talking, and Dr. Alster touched his arm. "You can go back to work, Joe," he said quietly.

"But if I am resigning—"

"You cannot resign—so go back on duty. I'll make a check later this afternoon, but I'll be right here the rest of the day."

Joe looked down at the printed papers. "Has my mother read this?" he asked.

"Of course not. Those are proofs, the article has not yet been printed."

"And then she will read it."

"Probably, yes. I don't know the circulation of the newspaper—but I hazard an estimate that less than a third will read or understand it."

"It's interesting. The third will identify the case, and then everyone . . . Isn't there some way we can prevent—not me, but you, sir—"

"He won't try," said Jane. She raised herself on tiptoe, looked over the hedge, and lifted a finger to Alster. "Murphy," her lips said silently.

Joe saw her. "Oh, Lord!" he groaned.

"Go back to work," said Alster firmly. "Your beeper is beeping."

"Why, sir—" Joe drew his silent beeper from his pocket and looked at it.

"Get going!" said Alster. "Right now! *Stat!* And immediately, besides." He took the proof sheets from Dr. Raithel's hand.

Murphy Anderson had evidently read the article. He nodded when he saw the proof strips Alster was holding. "Was Raithel resigning?" he asked.

"Trying to. I can't spare him," said Alster. "Now if it were Jane—"

"What did you do a thing like that for?" Murphy asked her.

"How did you get wind of it?"

"Lord, woman, no newspaper accepts a free-lance article without checking on its validity. I thought maybe you had told them to check it with me."

"I love you, too," said Jane, going up the steps to the house.

"Make us some limeade," Alster called after her. He turned back to Murphy. "Sit down. Why did you think Jane wanted you to see this thing?" he asked.

"She's proud of her sleuthing."

"Yes, she is. But her articles have got her into trouble before."

"The sand painting. Yes, I know."

"I think you might talk to Raithel."

"Didn't you?"

"You can drink your limeade, and go up there. What I said made very little impression."

"Mmmm. I'll see what I can do. He won't be upset about hurting my wife's feelings."

"I didn't do more than suggest the woman-scorned bit."

Murphy laughed and rose to take the tray from Jane's hands. "You look lovely this morning," he told her.

"It's two o'clock in the afternoon."

"The dew hangs on. How are the kids doing?"

"Alster says Mark is at work every day. That's all we know."

"Well, maybe you're having things lucky."

Jane shrugged. "Stick around," she said. "If you leave, Alster will beat me for writing that article."

"He should."

Murphy drank his limeade with relish. He said he wished Jane would stick to her culinary talents.

"Don't tell her a thing like that. I'd have TV dinners for a month."

"Where did she get her facts for this thing?"

Alster told him about the bag of pill bottles. "And she knew enough medicine to do the necessary research. She was burned up because Joe fell flat on his face over Margaret."

"After the publicity that he had helped create about his being smitten with Jane."

Alster laughed. "That's all it took. She even mentioned that he was nearer her—Jane's—age than he was Margaret's."

"She didn't want him."

"Do you expect her to be reasonable?"

"Well, not often. Does Raithel know I'm down here?"

"I don't believe he saw you come. I told him to get back to work."

"But you'd like me to talk to him."

"It might help. His ego gets flattened much too easily."

"Whose doesn't? Why don't you and Jane go to see the kids?"

"We haven't been invited."

"Oh, now look, Alster—"

"I shouldn't mention ego, should I?"

"No—of all people."

Alster waved his glass at his friend. "Go up and talk to Raithel. I called him a ninny the other day, and he surely can be. I think that's why you left the hospital."

"It was not." Murphy stood up, set his glass on the tray, and sighed. "I should have stayed at home," he said.

"Why didn't you?"

"Alan is learning to play the harmonica."

Alster chuckled and waved his friend away. "Go put some clothes on," Murphy heard him call to Jane. "We'll go see the kids."

*

"One good deed a day is enough," muttered Murphy, pushing the bar to open the hospital door.

There were visitors about; he was stopped a half-dozen times by people who had known him when he was the company medical officer—and half of them asked why he had left.

"So you would have the advantage of Dr. Alster." He found a good way to answer that. It did not encourage much further conversation.

He found Dr. Raithel in his own quarters. A small bedroom and a pleasant sitting room, which looked out across the parklike grounds, as did everything in the complex. Murphy rapped on the door frame.

Joe jumped to his feet. "Oh, Dr. Murphy!" he cried. "I mean Dr. Anderson. Come in, come in!"

"Thank you, I will."

He sat down on the corner of the couch. "Things seem fairly quiet around here," he said.

"They are. The only complaint has been about meat loaf for dinner."

"On Sunday? I should think so!"

"Last week they fussed because we have chicken every Sunday."

"You do keep things stirred up."

Joe sat down in the armchair, then stood up again. "Have you talked to Dr. Alster?" he asked.

"They have gone to see their daughter."

"Oh. I thought maybe—"

"I did. Alster showed me the article that Jane had written."

Joe rubbed his hands together. "I offered my resignation."

"Which, of course, he refused."

"But, Dr. Anderson—"

"If you did what the article says you did, you had no

choice but to make the offer. You don't really want to leave, do you?"

"No, sir, but—"

"You made a big boo-boo, my son."

"I know I did, sir. I wish—"

"That no one but you need know about it. Well, it is nice when we doctors can tuck our mistakes into our pockets, and forget them. But, Holy Moses, man, if we resigned each time we made one—"

"They don't all get written up in the newspaper."

"No, they don't."

"People will wonder why Dr. Alster doesn't kick me out."

"Do you wonder?"

"Well, it would leave him with all the work to do."

Murphy laughed. "And that might be an item with Alster. I can't really blame him for keeping you on."

Joe frowned. "But," he said uncertainly, "if he does keep me on, and the newspaper comes out with that article about misguided brotherly love, won't the company ask him why he keeps me?"

"No doubt he has thought of that."

Joe Raithel regarded the quiet-faced man in his tan linen shirt-jacket and trousers. One could not easily read Murphy Anderson's face.

"What will he say to them?" he asked. "He can't tell them that he doesn't want to do my work and his, too."

"Oh, it would not occur to him to say that. No, he would tell them that you do a very good job under orders. And you do, Joe."

This pleased the younger man, but slowly his smile faded. "Do you mean, sir," he asked, "that I would not be able to work on my own?"

"It means that you should be expending every effort

right now to learn while you have a good man to teach you!" Anderson's voice had sharpened.
 Joe nodded. "I am sure that is true," he said slowly. "Yet I am about persuaded that I cannot stay on here. If I killed my brother—"
 "Did you?"
 The question surprised Dr. Raithel. "I don't know. I didn't mean to. But I feel that just the chance that I did could force me to give up medicine."
 "And," said Murphy smoothly, "give you a reason, a chance to be free of your mother."
 Joe's eyes flared, and his cheeks turned scarlet. "Yes," he admitted. "I am afraid so. It is ungrateful of me."
 "I wouldn't say so. And if I have any advice for you, which you might want, and possibly use, I would tell you to stay here in this hospital, live here in your quarters, and do the medicine that is here to do. Learn what you can from Dr. Alster—"
 "He's a good man."
 "Yes, and he knows a lot. He also has learned that life cannot force him out of his chosen profession. That it should not."
 "Could it have?" asked Joe in surprise.
 "Many times. Whatever a man's profession, and especially in medicine, his personal life can bother him. It has bothered Alster. It has bothered me. Don't you remember that it was Alan's vandalism against a patient that took me away from the position that Alster now holds? But a man cannot let these personal interferences change the main channel of his life. Running away does no good. I withdrew from institutional medicine, but I kept my profession."
 "Do you like private practice?"
 "Yes. And it seems to be working out." Murphy stood

up. "You think on these things, my son. Did I tell you that Alster had gone to see his daughter?"

"And he'll probably not be back until bed check."

"That's right. So I'll be getting about my own business instead of attending to yours."

"I am grateful, Dr. Anderson."

"I hope we can keep it that way."

Joe watched the tall man go down the driveway to the street, and he decided to check the floor desks before eating his supper. The phone was ringing in Dr. Alster's office and he went in to answer it. He told the caller that the chief was gone for the day. "You might try calling back about eight," he said. "Here, or at his home."

Why hadn't the man's answering service . . . ? He set the phone down, saw that the top drawer was open a bit, and with the hand that would have closed it, automatically locking it, he pulled it open far enough to see the bottle that it contained. He rolled the thing over, closed the drawer, shrugged, and went out into the hall.

"I am going to make rounds," he told the nurse in charge.

"Yes, doctor. Our only new patient is that tonsillectomy."

It was a quiet week. "Before the storm?" Alster asked Jane.

"After, perhaps. In comparison with what we've had. Funerals and weddings . . ."

"I wonder if the kids ever drank all that carrot juice."

"Would it hurt them?"

"We've had no admissions."

On Friday night he was able to tell, and make his

friends laugh, about their visit to the "children's" house. Sawed into four pieces, put back together with a stapling gun, furnished with things from Goodwill—"You never did see such a hall tree!"—and with some wedding-gift money they had bought a second-hand generator to provide lights. "Yes, it works. I'll say it works!" They had also bought a bushel of carrots and a juicer—not a blender, mind you, but a juicer—and had extracted the juice from those damn carrots. "From the color, I'd say they had not washed them."

"Oh, but they did," said Jane. "Margaret told me they had cleaned them with a pot scrubber. You should have seen Alster's face when he was offered a glass of the juice."

Everyone laughed. Helen Cobb said it sounded as if the kids were doing all right.

This was a special dinner. It was Eric Pemscot's birthday, and he had requested that everyone in the group be present. Kate Beetz and Helen Cobb had baked a cake that was marked off into the exact number of pieces. Kate had prepared the greens for a wilted-lettuce salad Eric especially liked, though the chef protested with her. He could have made the salad. And the cake, too, for that matter.

It was a gay party. The members had dressed, the women in pretty, long-skirted gowns, the men in suits and ties. Eric was very pleased, and Dan Cobb was already showing the effects of his third martini when . . .

"Oh, oh!" said Hilda Curren.

The group, as usual, was eating at a long table out in a glassed-in porch, which was like an alcove to the main dining room.

Now, at Hilda's warning, all eyes turned to the woman who was making her way between the smaller tables of the big room, gayly greeting those she knew, smiling at everyone. In contrast to the flowery prints and pale pastels of the other women's frocks, the tall, slender woman wore black. A long dress, its pleated ruffle rippling. The bodice was minimal, but she had pretty arms and shoulders; a gauzy scarf was drawn lightly through her bent elbows.

"Oquist," said Alster gruffly, but loudly enough for the uninvited guest to hear.

"Now, doctor," she chided him. She went, undulating, behind the chairs and the people seated in them, to where Eric Pemscot sat. "I came to surprise you on your birthday!" she announced. The men, somewhat reluctantly, were rising to their feet.

Except for Alster, no one had spoken. Now Eric said stiffly, "Sit down, gentlemen. This was not designed to be a surprise party."

He stepped away when Rose would have kissed him. Helen and Kate looked meaningly at the cake, a candle on each wedge. "There's no room for an extra chair," murmured Helen.

"The lady," said the waitress, "tole me she pay for the whole party."

Now everyone did look at Rose. How could a non-member . . . ?

"Eric's signed the check," said Jane. "I saw him do it. Though we meant to be giving the party for him."

"And not his girl friend?" asked Rose archly.

"Pure brass!" said Alice Denby.

Rose flashed her a glance that should have singed. Alster stepped away from the table. He took Rose's arm. "Let me help you, Miss Oquist," he said smoothly. "There has been a mix-up of some sort. I am sure Mr. Pemscot will get in touch with you."

"Not if I can stop him," said Helen Cobb. They all

watched the firm, pleasant way in which Alster got the woman between the tables and the more-than-interested people in the dining room.

Within ten minutes he returned. "Now, where was I?" he asked.

"You were calling Rose *Oquist,*" drawled Jane.

"Oh? I thought I was talking about carrot juice and our children."

"Did you and Jane walk down to where they are living?" asked Hilda, ready to help change the subject.

"No, we drove as close as we could get, then packed in."

"*Packed?*"

"I am acquiring a whole new vocabulary. Not necessarily better. And we did go through a deal of underbrush and fallen timber to get to where they have reassembled that house. I believe Mark feels that they went to considerable and unnecessary labor. He looks up and around their little clearing, he sees nothing but trees, trees, trees, which his modern-day mind converts into so many board feet of lumber.

"And Alster spent an hour . . ." Jane offered.

"Let me finish it," Murphy broke in. "Alster spent an hour trying to convince his carrot-drinking son-in-law that there is no real reason why everything on this earth with a dollar value should be sold and destroyed."

Alster's head had gone up sharply, and his hawklike gaze was fastened upon Murphy. "Why must you be the one to force home to me," he asked, "that I have a loathsome thing called a son-in-law?"

Murphy shrugged. "Someone has always had to teach you the facts of life," he drawled.

"And without them—"

"You would be a funny old man indeed."

Laughter exploded all around the table. Alster sat

down, ate his salad, and refused to talk any more about his "children," or people named Oquist. It turned out to be a pretty good party. Someone out in the bar began to play the piano and everyone decided to dance. Anne Hother pointed out that Rose would have just made an odd person. "Murphy and Eric bachelors—Hilda and Kate and—no, it doesn't come out right, does it?"

"Besides, I am not going to dance with Anderson," said Eric. And, by that time, the group could laugh at that. So it was a good party.

It was a couple of days later that Murphy came to Alster's office late in the afternoon.

"Don't you have a waiting room full of patients?" Dr. Alster asked him.

"I did have, but with my usual efficiency and dispatch—"

"Then why aren't you playing golf? You are destroying the public image of us pill-pushers."

Murphy settled into the patient's chair, and began to make a chain from the little box of paper clips on Alster's desk. "I don't play golf, and I have a thing on my mind."

Alster signed his name on a paper, which he cracked into a tray on the far side of his desk. "Only one thing?"

"No, but over this one I believe I can stir up a row with you."

"And you love to do that, don't you?"

"I do. It cleans out all the arteries and canals of my brain."

Alster waited. "I am referring," Murphy obliged him by saying, "to the unquenchable rumor that Joe Raithel murdered his brother."

"He was here in Baumgarten, and had been for weeks, when the man died."

"I know that, but the rumor says, one version does, that he prescribed the wrong medicine."

Alster was reading another paper, his pen poised. "Have you been talking to Rose Oquist?" he asked.

"I wish to God, Alster, you would not deliberately antagonize people like that woman!"

"I antagonize you, and you aren't one bit like Rose."

Murphy grunted. "Rose Oquest, with the help of others, is behind the rumors going around."

"Rumors about Joe?"

"And you."

Alster's head went up sharply. "What have *I* done?" he demanded. "What do your rumors say that I've done? I have never *seen* Joe Raithel's brother."

"But you are here in the company hospital. You pass out orders to Joe. And among them you have been telling him what the doctors should have been doing for his brother."

Alster drew his lips into a thin line.

"You knew there were rumors?"

"I've known more about that than you do."

"Alster . . ."

"I thought I could squash it before you or very many others could hear about it."

Murphy stood up and leaned across the desk. "Did you," he demanded, "really let Margaret go through that ridiculous wedding to keep her from marrying Joe Raithel?"

Alster tipped back in his chair, his face dead white. "What in hell are you talking about, Murphy? I didn't want Margaret to marry anyone, ridiculous or not. Is that Oquist woman starting *that* sort of talk? Joe and Margaret—those two barely knew each other! My God! Where do I start on this?"

"You could start by not getting into such things, Alster."

Alster leaned forward again, fished his keys from his

pocket, and unlocked the top drawer of his desk. Murphy put his hand over the top of the foam cup. "That won't help," he said sternly. "Tell me your side of this mess."

Alster glared at him. "I don't have any side," he shouted. "I got into this 'thing,' as you call it, unknowingly. Innocently. The same way I got into Jane's name in purple graffiti on that building downtown. Margaret came home announcing that she was going to marry Mark, and neither I nor anyone else could stop her. Joe Raithel had a mortally sick brother three hundred miles away, and the man died. Maybe Joe was smitten with my daughter. A lot of young men have been. But beyond fathering her—"

Now he was on his feet. Murphy stood back, his face watchful. "What in hell should I do about all this, Murphy?" Alster cried.

"I think you know what you should do."

"You know about the article Jane wrote?"

"Of course. It takes more than a rumor to make me close down my office in midafternoon."

"Uh-huh! Then I do know what I should do first."

He went to the closet, changed his white jacket for a seersucker one. "I'd better kill that article, hadn't I?" he asked.

"You'd like me to do it, wouldn't you?"

"Would you?" Alster's face brightened.

Murphy shook his head. "Though I know you are afraid of Jane."

Alster opened the door. "I am," he said firmly.

"Me, too," said Murphy, following him. "She's what keeps me single."

Alster checked out at the desk, and the two men left the hospital, walking long-legged down the drive to the street and along it toward the main part of the little town. Automatically, they spoke to people they passed.

"Is Jane," asked Alster curiously, "the only fear you have?"

Murphy avoided a small child on a tricycle. "Oh, no, indeed," he said.

"Nor me," Alster agreed.

"Do you know where we are going?"

Alster pointed his hand across the street intersection to the building that housed the local newspaper.

"Jees," breathed Murphy.

"Have to go to the source," Alster said.

The editor of this small but excellent newspaper was a white-haired gentleman with the pink skin of a baby, and the bland, if not so innocent, blue eyes. He was surprised, but evidently pleased, to receive what he chose to call the "city's medical luminaries."

"If that doesn't go any farther than this office, we'll accept the title," said Murphy, sitting down on a chair.

The editor resumed his place before his cluttered, rolltop desk. The Baumgarten newspaper survived by being a better paper, and more widely read, than that of Scott, the larger town.

Murphy nodded to Alster, who smoothed one hand with the other. "I understand," he said, "that my wife has offered you, for publication, an article on leukemia and aplastic anemia."

"She has offered me an article," the editor agreed. "It is more personal than professional."

"And has to do with the thwarted, perhaps misguided, love of one brother for another."

The editor nodded. "That would state its gist," he agreed.

"Are you going to print it?"

"I have it in proof." He rummaged among the papers

on his desk and brought out the long galley. Alster waved it away. "Give it to Murphy," he said. "I've read the thing."

"Mrs. Alster writes very well."

"But without tact and discretion," said Alster dryly. "She tells me that she has researched her material . . ."

"Oh, she did. And she uses no names—which she scarcely needs to do around here. Did you pay her for this article?"

"Our usual ten cents a line for free lancing. It isn't much."

"I'll buy it back at fifteen."

The editor laughed. "You don't want the article printed?"

"And before you're done with it, you'll wish it had not been published."

"I have to sell newspapers, doctor. This column would justify a five-thousand-run paper."

"Jane got her facts entirely by accident."

"Did the man give his brother the wrong medicine?"

"He made a false diagnosis. We all do that. Me, Dr. Anderson, Dr. Raithel."

"And you don't want your patients to know that."

Alster laughed dryly. "I don't want it set down in print." He took the galley from Murphy. "She calls this thing 'The Love of a Brother.' Yes. And then, using her small knowledge of medicine, and my files, she hypothecates that such a love can be lethal."

The editor leaned dangerously back in his chair and rolled the galley strip around two fingers. "Tell me this, Dr. Alster," he said, "is it difficult for a doctor, even a competent one, to hand over a member of his family to the care of another M.D.?"

Murphy and Alster exchanged glances. "It is difficult," said Alster readily. "I remember when I thought Margaret should have her tonsils out. Murph here was her doctor of record. He disagreed with me and refused to do the surgery. I was sure she would be deaf if he didn't do it. We two fought like rolling cats over the matter."

"I didn't take out the tonsils," said Murphy, "and Margaret has keen hearing. Too keen at times."

"And you and Dr. Alster remain friends."

"We still fight like rolling cats," Alster assured him.

The editor unrolled his bit of newsprint. "I'd like a five-thousand run," he mused.

"Sure you would. But look, I can give you an article as a swap."

"Would Mrs. Alster write it?"

"She could. She keeps my records." And he told about the cholesterol experiments.

The editor agreed it had interest. "But not the personal angle," he pointed out.

"Are you in competition with the *National Weekly,* or whatever it is called? 'Who slept in whose bed last night?'"

The editor laughed and shook his head. "But I would enjoy their circulation," he admitted.

Murphy stood up. "Can't you tell us what you are ready to do?" he asked. "This thing can grow . . ."

"I know that. And you fellows want me to agree to do what I can to prevent its growth. My stand is to wait a while and see—sometimes these things die of their own weight."

"Or they get watered and sunshined in the press. Watering does nasty things to dynamite."

"Yes, it does, Murphy. And the first one hurt will be this young doctor. He seems like a nice chap."

"He is," said Alster, "and he will learn his lesson in this happening, without your publishing that account of brotherly love. I'll see that he learns it. I'll show him the ethical, and possibly legal, wrong of substituting another medicine for that ordered by the doctor in charge of a patient. I'll crack down hard on him, sir."

"He will, too," Murphy confirmed. "Alster's talent is perhaps that of teaching young doctors how to heel-and-toe down the medical pathways. And while you're at it, Alster—"

The dark, slender man nodded. "I'll give him some pertinent facts about talk and how it can affect a medic, and I might even just lecture him about another member of his family. You know, his mother brought those medicine bottles to our house, put them into Jane's hands. There is a good chance she guessed what might be done with them."

The editor's face turned purple. "Oh, we couldn't play along with that!" he cried.

"She may really have been proud of Joe and wanted his efforts to save his brother publicized . . ."

"I wouldn't go along with that, either," said the editor firmly.

The two doctors prepared to leave. "What are you going to tell Jane?" Alster asked curiously.

"That next week we plan pages and pages on the forestry business, and by then her material will be useless to us."

"Alster can quote Thoreau for you," said Murphy maliciously.

"If you ever find him dead under a hedge," said Alster smoothly, "don't seek to question why."

Murphy laughed. "Sir," he said to the editor, "take up his offer on the cholesterol thing, and besides that I might be coaxed to write something for you."

"About medicine?" asked the editor. "People are always interested in that."

"I know," said Murphy. "But my inspiration is to do something about doctors' families."

"Whooo-whooo!" breathed Alster. "You like that better than Jane's effort, don't you?" he asked the editor.

"If he could make it a series . . ."

"He could; he would." Alster reached for the unrolled galley.

The editor saw him put it into his pocket. And he sighed a little. "You're right, of course," he agreed. "I can't use that thing."

8

Out on the sidewalk, Alster bade Murphy good-bye and moved toward the complex and the hospital. By that time the light was changing, quickly softening as it did in these forested mountains. Sunlight still gilded the upper slopes, but in the valley—he turned sharply and struck out for the wooded hills.

"Wherein lies my strength," he muttered to himself. And it did. He would need strength, to tell Jane what was what about her article, to think a little about anything he might write, or suggest that she write, to consider Murphy. Would he really write something? He could, all right.

And just to think of the past days, of Joe Raithel, and Margaret's wedding, about her belonging to that big young man—

He walked, and he thought.

Jane had seen the two doctors leave the hospital and walk toward town. It was earlier than Alster usually made rounds and left the hospital. Murphy must have had something for them to do together. They would be back by dinnertime, she was fairly certain, and as a reward she would make some fresh bread. Or rolls. Murphy especially liked that. Alster did, too, but he watched his weight. He was not as muscular as Murphy.

Anyway . . .

She was wearing a yellow jump suit, and she tied a protective apron around her waist. She reached for the bowls and pans she would need—she greased her hands, closed the stopper of one sink, and put cold water into it so that she could get her rings off easily. Usually she closed both sinks, but today she was hurrying, to give the dough time to rise, and—

She screamed. Not loudly, but breathily, almost a whistling intake of breath. Her rings had come off quickly all right, but one of them—the diamond engagement ring Alster had given her eighteen years ago—a handsome solitaire—a white diamond of which she was very proud—that ring had gone into the other sink, the one she had not closed, and down into the disposal. Automatically, in her fright, she touched the switch, only for a moment. It whirred, it groaned, and she shut it off. Why had she done that? Why *had* she? White-faced, she stared down at the open circle of the disposal. She forced her hand down into it, the plate would not turn—

What in heaven's name would she tell Alster? He would kill her. Literally, he would kill her. Oh . . . She wiped her hands on a towel. She put away the pans and the bowls, the flour, the jar of yeast starter—but she kept looking at the disposal; the wedding ring lay to one side and she put it on.

Murphy had been with Alster; she could not call him for advice. She supposed she could call one of the maintenance men from the plant. Maybe one of her friends—Kate, or Hilda—would have an idea. A jeweler—no, that was ridiculous.

Could the disposal be disconnected from underneath? She knelt down and surveyed the round cylinder under the sink. What *was* she to do? She could not face Alster—and yet she wished he would come home. He would know . . .

If she could just *talk* to somebody! Margaret simply must have a phone put in so her mother could talk to her. Mark might be able—could she run all the way up to where they lived, and get back before Alster . . . ?

If she just had not touched that switch! But she was so upset to see her ring go down into that black hole—oh, Alster would be right! She was crazy. She didn't think.

And now—

The telephone rang, and she answered it; she snapped at the woman who was selling aluminum siding—

Through the glass wall, she saw Joe Raithel come down the slope, a jacket over swim trunks. He gestured to the pool, and she waved her hand to signal permission to use it. His mother probably would know, but Mrs. Raithel despised her. Jane knew that she did. She was afraid—

For some reason she went upstairs and changed from the jump suit into a green and white skirt, a green blouse. She guessed she was doing what little she could to keep Alster's temper down. He allowed pants on women, but he really didn't like them.

In between all these things, she frequently pushed her hand down into the disposal in the hope that she had missed feeling the ring. The back of her hand was getting pink, and there was a scrape or two. She—

Joe finished his swim and went up to the hospital again, waving to her. She waved back, preoccupied. She walked about the house; she decided that she hated her pretty kitchen, and she knew that Alster would be home at any minute; he would immediately know that something had happened. He'd think of Margaret and start right up the hill—

But—oh, glory, here came Murphy! Alone, and right up to their door, big as a tree, strong and capable—he'd tell Alster, of course, but he would help her, too. She let him in, and dissolved into tears. He was alarmed, and, of course, thought of Margaret—where was Alster? Yes, they had been together earlier that afternoon—but that was two hours ago . . .

"Now, look, Jane. Settle down and tell me what has happened." He brought her a glass of water, the tap was turned to drain into the empty sink. She sat down on one of the chairs and he stood between her and the window, firm as a rock, his face alert but impassive. Her words tumbled out, and he made her go over the story three or four times. Had she baked the ring into the bread?

"Oh, damn the bread!" cried Jane. "I was only getting ready to mix it. I thought you would come back with Alster, and you both like hot bread, and—I saw you go off somewhere together."

"Yes, we had an errand downtown. I thought—isn't he at the hospital?"

"I don't know. He hasn't come home—"

"Haven't you called him?"

"No. I was afraid he would be so furious. If I could get the ring out before he comes—"

Gradually he discovered that her diamond ring had gone down the disposal; she had turned the switch on for just a second—

"Why?"

She ran her hands through her hair. She didn't know, either, why she hadn't closed both sinks.

He nodded. "I know a plumber . . ." he said. "There

just might be a chance—though I think Alster should be in on this. I'll call the hospital first."

This he did. Dr. Alster would be back about eight. Was there a message?

Then he dialed another number. "We'll have to wait until he gets here," he told Jane. "He's a good man. If anyone can help you— Now you come in and sit down, try to calm yourself."

She went in and she sat down; Murphy watched her in concern. He took out his penlight and looked into the disposal. "Nothing," he told her.

And finally the man came, a plumber.

He greeted Dr. Anderson as a friend and asked what had happened—complex maintenance on strike?

"This is a personal job for me, Gene," Murphy told the man, and he introduced him to Jane.

Gene was impressed. "It's a pleasure," he said. "And you sure do have a pretty kitchen."

"I used to think so," said Jane. "Murph, will you tell him?"

"I think I'd better," agreed Dr. Anderson.

The plumber—his name was Gene Grey—listened quietly, glancing now and then at Jane. He was a solid, stocky man, about forty, with a pleasant, quiet manner. He whistled softly when he heard what had happened.

"I never before had left both sinks unstopped," said Jane, her voice trembling.

"And the first time was the wrong time," said Mr. Grey quietly. "All right. Let's see what we have here."

He wore a wide leather belt to which were affixed various tools in leather cases. Among them was a flashlight, and with it in hand, he approached the sink.

He brushed aside a frond of greenery from a hanging basket, ready to use the strong flashlight; he looked over his shoulder at Jane. "You know," he warned, "the ring already could be in splinters." He cut the rubbery fringe from the circle of the disposal, then he drew a long-bladed screwdriver from his belt, and with the light in the disposal, he used the tool to turn the blades slowly, very slowly—

Murphy and Jane watched him breathlessly. They saw his shoulders relax—just a fraction.

"You've found it!" Jane cried. "You've *found* it!"

"Take it easy, lady. I see it. At least there's a flash. Wait a minute—I may have to—" He was all concentration again, bent over the sink.

He gestured to Murphy. "Can you pull my long-nosed pliers out, Doc? I always did know I should have had three hands."

Murphy found the pliers.

Then Gene took his hand and placed it on the flashlight. "Hold it just exactly there, Doc. Where I can see the fish I'm after."

It took only a minute, perhaps two, but slowly, then firmly, triumphantly, the ring was pulled out. Jane reached her hand for it. But Gene held it beyond her reach, examining it under the bright beam of the flashlight. The platinum circle of the ring was bent—"That caught the brunt of the blade—" said Gene, "—and there may be a chip, but I think you were very lucky, Mrs. Alster. That's a beautiful diamond." He handed it to Murphy, who examined it and then gave it to Jane.

"You'll have to take it to the jeweler's," he said.

Jane held the ring tight in her clenched fist. "Oh, I shall, I shall. Mr. Grey—"

"I'll send you a bill," said the plumber, assembling his tools. He patted the ceramic dog on the head and walked out. "The company maintenance man maybe can replace the baffle," he called over his shoulder.

200

"*Adios,* Doc," he called to Murphy.

"He thinks I'm a fool," said Jane.

"He knows all kinds."

"Humph," said Jane, wrapping the ring in tissue paper. "You won't need to tell Alster about this, will you?"

"I won't need to, but you will."

"He'll kill me," said Jane solemnly.

"Now why should he do that? You have the ring. He'll know about it when he gets the bill for its repair. Why should you, why *do* you, do things behind his back, Jane? Secretly. That is what infuriates him."

"I have some rights as a woman."

"You do. And as a wife. But Alster has rights, too. Give the man a chance, girl. Give him a chance."

Jane found her purse and tucked the diamond ring into it. "Now!" she said. "I'll have to think what I'll do for dinner. You don't like Alster," she said to Dr. Anderson, who was seated at the table watching her. "That's why—"

"I do like Alster," he broke in, his tone firm. "I disagree with him often, and you can. But we are friends. I have my rights, and he has his. Friendship is much like a marriage, Jane, my dear . . ."

"I can think of differences."

"There are some. But both relationships require trust and respect between two people."

"And that's how you feel about Alster. Do you like salmon salad?"

"I like it, but I am not staying for dinner."

She turned, her eyes flashing. He stretched a hand toward her.

"Are you afraid of Alster, Jane?" he asked gently.

"Of course I'm afraid of him. And you are, too."

"No," said Murphy. "Not in any way."

201

"Well, I am."

"He loved you when he gave you that ring."

"He loved me when he gave me Margaret. We've stayed together on her account, and sex has been a part of it. But now—when something like this happens—"

"He admires your mind. He says you do a fine job of keeping his records on the research he's interested in."

"A woman wants more. Though I suppose, as Doc said, I am really too old to excite a man. And I should take what I can claim."

Murphy was smiling. "You know damn well you excite men."

She took a step toward him. Her eyes were wide and shining.

He laughed and stood up.

"Don't try it on me, Jane. I have a job I want to work on with Alster."

"I could help, perhaps."

"Not in this, I think."

"It won't ever work with you, will it, Murph?"

"I don't know. What *works?* Really? I suppose it's the trying that matters."

"And you won't try."

"Because I know I'd get into the most ungodly mess of my ungodly life."

She nodded. "But it's fun to play just a hand or two in the game. You like it when I flirt with you."

"Of course I do, knowing all the time that it's the playing of the game that counts. Considering that life is a bridge tournament—"

"Oh, for heaven's sake!" cried Jane. *"Bridge tournaments—"*

"You find them inviting. You like the thought of a new deck, a new partner—"

Her eyes lifted. "And a new opponent."

"You bet. The chance of success, the chance of failure."

"But that's life, Murphy!"

"What else is there?"

"Salmon salad for dinner."

He went past her, slapping her shoulder as he passed her. "I had it for lunch," he drawled. " 'Bye, sweetheart. Better freshen your makeup. Alster will need a little seduction when you tell him about the ring."

The next day Alster worked, his mind evidently preoccupied. He performed surgery; he examined a man who might have hepatitis, and isolated him. Over lunch he talked to Joe Raithel about the young doctor's future plans. "You aren't apt to take my job away from me," he said. "Even if I fall dead, or leave for another staff, I don't think you'd get it. Why don't you apply for a residency in some big center, and specialize? You're at a dead end here."

"I am realizing that, Dr. Alster. I couldn't take full charge here if you left—"

"No, there isn't much opportunity for me to give you authority. You're a good doctor, Joe. You know what's what. The thing you need now is to be chief resident of a ward full of patients, all of them ready to give trouble. That will teach you judgment and give you the guts you need."

"Will you help me find such a place?"

"I'd give you good recommendations when you find your own place."

"What will you do here?"

"Find another Joe Raithel."

"I guess there are plenty of us."

"There are. You might try taking one of the small-town clinic jobs offered in the *Journal*. You'd get your guts there."

"And judgment, too?"

"Pretty quick, pretty quick."

"Did Mrs. Alster take her ring into Scott, or is she . . . ?"

Alster looked up. "How did you hear about that?"

"I was down at the pool. Jane flew all to pieces. Dr. Anderson was there, and a plumber came from Scott. I learned later that she had lost her ring down the drain. Was it a real diamond, doctor?"

Alster stared at him, then smiled. "Do you think I'd give my wife a fake one?"

"No, but everyone has commented on the size of that one."

"And speculated on its genuineness." He stood up. "Sorry I asked how you knew about the matter. In this town, and this hospital, there are no secrets."

"In your home, too, sir. With walls of glass, I could see what was being done."

Alster nodded. "My apologies. Of course you saw the row about the ring." He walked out of the dining room. There was to be a staff meeting at four and he had many things to do.

But he thought—about the ring, of course, and when Murphy showed up he asked him if losing it, almost losing it, was all that important.

"Didn't you make the row Jane expected?"

"I told her it was a damned expensive ring."

"Oh, yes. I remember when it was called Dick Alster's folly."

Alster snorted. "And Jane knows she may have to live on it some day."

"But you didn't make a row?"

"Not the one she expected. I felt sure she had fore-

204

seen one bigger than any I could make. But I did get pretty nasty about her journalism."

Murphy laughed. "I suspect she did not like that."

"She did not. Why did you visit us yesterday?"

"I had this letter for you. Sent to me rather than through your office here."

"Word gets around, doesn't it?" drawled Alster, reading the letter. "My guardian angel, my nemesis—my—" He broke off to whistle and look sharply at Murphy. "Did you tell Jane about this?" he asked.

"No. Anyway, she was throwing rocks down the disposal, and making salmon salad and stuff. I had a carbon, of course."

"Yes." Alster put the letter back into the envelope and tapped it against his other hand.

"You are doing some very good work on your cholesterol project," Murphy told him.

"It would seem so. But it got me fired from the VA."

"I know. You did it at a bad time. They were being sensitive about using the vets as guinea pigs. That's the way these things happen."

"It's the way everything happens," said Alster wryly. "It is not what a man does, it's what affects his personal life, or what's in the newspapers that matters. Movie actors learn that, and doctors do. Politicians."

"And it happens to be Dick Alster's vulnerable point," said Murphy, laughing. "I have to get back to work. Congrats, and all that."

"Mmmm. I have some work to do myself."

He did the work. He read and reread the letter. And at four o'clock, spic and span in fresh whites, he went across to the conference room.

In his turn, he made his report: patients, expenses, and the latest results of the cholesterol tests.

"You seem to be doing good work there, Doctor," said Mr. Pemscot kindly.

Alster nodded. "Maybe," he agreed.

The whole thing seemed to be routine, and he let his thoughts drift. Or, at least, instead of considering only the matter being discussed, he also thought about something else, the letter in his pocket, his visit with the kids the day before, and—and—

He sat erect. What was *this?* The hospital here in Baumgarten closed? Phased out was the term. Consolidated with the company's central unit for long-term injuries or illnesses. Emergencies to be handled at the two hospitals in Scott, with only a dispensary here. The building would be used for—

He stood up. "I know walking papers when I see them waved under my nose!" he cried.

"Oh, sit down, Alster," said Pemscot.

"Why should I?"

"For one thing, this move will take six months at least."

"Ten minutes ago you were praising our research project."

"That can be continued."

"The hell it can!" He heard his ugly tone. But here he was, right back to his dismissal from the VA. "If I'm not the company doctor, men won't be available for testing," he pointed out. "And where in the devil will that doctor be working? This certainly has not been the perfect setup for me, but I planned to stick it out. Because of the setting, and the chance to do research. And I just may remind you that I have a year's contract."

"We are well aware of that, doctor. A year's contract with a five-year option of renewal. And you are not being fired, sir! We—as I've said—we expect it to take six months to close the facility here."

"The hospital, as such."

"Yes, sir. And that would about wind up the contract you mentioned. Then, on your option, you could go to the central offices."

"And *facilities*." Alster's voice was still acid. "That would mean Minnesota, I suppose."

"Yes, sir, it would."

"Or I could take over the dispensary here."

"Now, *Doctor!*"

"I'm sorry, Pemscot. You caught me off base."

"Could we offer the dispensary position to Dr. Raithel?"

"You could offer it, but I believe he is already thinking of a move away from this sort of situation."

"Well, that too can be taken care of during the six months we have. I can assure you the company's record of taking care of its people will see that he is placed."

Dr. Alster sat down, his thoughts churning. He remembered that, at the time of his severance from the Veterans Administration, Jane had suggested that he talk to Mike, his son. Should he do that now? At that time he had said something about one's children never understanding the father's work. Now was he ready to admit that the father himself often did not understand it? And that he could get pretty low trying to do it?

At a break in the procedure, he punctiliously asked if he might be excused. He had rounds to make.

He did make them. He kept an appointment he had made earlier with a detail man. Then he changed his clothes and disappeared.

9

Alster did not return until Jane had given up and gone to bed. During the evening there had been telephone calls; Joe Raithel came, all in a tizzy over the hospital closing—Jane went into something of a tizzy herself. But Alster was called out early the next morning and she had no chance to talk to him; before noon his secretary called with two messages. Would Mrs. Alster take her ring to a certain jeweler in Scott for possible repair, and plan to go to the country club for dinner? Yes, about seven.

"A party?" asked Jane. Surely they would not be saying good-bye so soon.

"The doctor just said dinner, Mrs. Alster."

Jane went to Scott; the jeweler thought he could reset the diamond so that the chip would not show. Possibly with other jewels? Yes, he understood she preferred a solitaire, well, with a new, pronged setting, as used these days, perhaps— No, the old band was beyond use.

Uncertain about how to dress, Jane called the club. Dr. Alster had reserved a table for three. So there would be no party.

"Did he order a menu?"

"He suggested king crab."

"Thank you." So she would not "dress," though she did put on a white silk blouse with a long skirt of blue and green print, a string of blue donkey beads around her throat. She pinned her pale hair back with a matching comb.

"You look fine," said Alster when he whirled in at fifteen minutes to seven. "I'll shower," he said, as he went up the steps.

He could dress in five minutes, and did that night, coming down in dark-blue trousers and a plaid jacket. On the way to the club Jane tried to talk to him about the hospital, but he said they would discuss their plans later. What about the ring? He thought she might use some smaller diamonds she had in other jewelry, and have a better setting. They discussed this even while being shown to their round table before a window overlooking the golf course. There were daisies in a clear cut vase, and glasses of sangria were served at once. The trees were darkening with shadows, and the evening was warm.

"Jane pointed to the third chair, her eyebrows up.

"Murph," said Alster, tasting the wine.

"You *asked* him?"

"I did."

"Why? He always shows up anyway."

"Now, Jane . . ."

"Well, he does."

"Often to our advantage."

"I think he's just plain nosy."

"In my opinion, the man is lonely."

"And he loves us?" Jane laughed aloud.

"I don't know about love, but we have become his family. And you were very glad to see him yesterday."

Through the rim of the glass held to her lips, Jane

looked at him. "Yesterday?" she repeated. "Oh! The ring! Yes, he was a help."

"I should say so." Alster was rising, and Jane turned to see Dr. Anderson approaching. He wore plaid slacks and a blue denim jacket stitched in white.

"*Wheee!*" she said. "Maybe I was wrong. This *is* a party!"

Murphy said it was, and the company good. They drank their sangria and watched returning golfers come across the grass. Only about half the tables in the dining room were occupied. Theirs had almost complete privacy.

"Some day," said Jane, confronted by her crab, "I'm going to cook and get the meat out of one of these creatures myself. They make delicious salad."

"It's much easier to buy a can," said Murphy, "and about as cheap."

"Well, with Alster out of a job . . ." she murmured. "Of course you know that he's been dumped again."

"I did not know he had been dumped, oh loyal wife of my friend," said Murphy dryly. "But I do know that the opportunity has come for us to offer that same friend a chance—no, to issue an invitation to him, to join me in my office practice."

Alster put down his slender fork and touched his napkin to his lips. Jane leaned toward Murphy. "You don't mean to work in your office!" she cried. "You *can't* mean that!"

"Why can't I? Alster's been doing pretty general practice as well as surgery this past six months."

"But you two *fight!*"

Alster and Murphy exchanged glances. Alster picked up his fork again. "We don't *fight*," said Murphy. "We disagree sometimes."

"You do," Jane agreed.

"He could have affiliations with both hospitals in Scott—and, yes, we do disagree. But we have done, and would do, good work together. Fight, if you choose that word, out solutions to our problems, do some research—"

"But not the cholesterol thing."

"Yes, he could do that, too. In the first place, it is not a *thing*. It is an important study. And, just this week, Alster's been offered a grant from the poultry industry to be sure he will continue it."

Jane was stunned. She stared at Murphy, then she stared at her husband. "Is that true?"

"Yes, of course it's true."

"How big a grant? Why didn't you tell me?"

"You threw your ring down the disposal."

"Oh, Alster—"

"You did. Murphy came to the house with the letter offering me the grant. And you had started such a hell of a fuss—"

"All right, all right. How big is the grant?"

"Big enough to clear up some of our problems—pay for the ring and a few other items. Of course I am hoping you won't stir up some more very soon."

She waved a crab claw at him. "I won't. I'm leaving town in a day or two."

"To go where?" asked Alster, not overly excited.

"Oh," said Jane airily, "I sent that chloromycetin article to a magazine, and they bought it."

The two men leaned toward her. "But you sold it to the newspaper!" they cried in unison.

"I know, but I'll take it back from them, now that—"

"Jane, you cannot, you simply cannot, offer a manuscript for sale to two editors at once."

"I didn't think both editors would buy it. Anyway, I am going to tell the editor of the Baumgarten newspaper that he can't have it."

"If he won't sell, may I suggest that you get your terms right? It was chlor . . ."

"I *know*," she said in exasperation. "I have it spelled correctly in the typescript."

"And you sold it to a magazine."

She was very pleased; her face glowed.

"And you are leaving town. For New York, I suppose?"

"Well, they said they would put me on their list of staff writers. To supply medical articles, correct other manuscripts, and so forth. You could come with me, of course."

"Thank you," said Alster dryly. "I'd be useful keeping you from saying chloromycetin when you mean chloramphenicol."

And both men laughed, not softly. Jane was hurt. "You never think I can do anything," she protested.

"I don't think you can base a life in New York on one short article sold," said Alster firmly.

"Then what will you do?"

"Well, let us both consider Murphy's offer. You seem to think we won't work well together."

"You do fight."

"All right. I'll grant you that we often disagree, and will. You may go to New York, if you must, and can do it at your own expense. As for me, without knowing of Murphy's offer, I was planning to use the six months I have at the complex and in their house to get my own life in order."

"You won't consider Murphy's offer?"

"I may. I certainly may if he is serious about it. For instance, Murph, is there work enough in your office for both of us?"

"Yes, and a divergence. If the complex hospital shuts down here, there will be a surge, both in the hospital occupancy in Scott and in outpatient care. The town will need our office, and the hospitals will welcome our availability for their staffs."

"You're sure of that."

"It just makes sense."

"I guess it does. And you're right. I could continue the cholesterol research, probably branch off into other things. All right then, tell me this. Is six months long enough to have a house built for me?"

"Not in your canyon," said Jane quickly.

He glanced at her. "You're living in New York, remember."

"I'll go there, but I probably can do my writing from any house you'll build."

"Do you have an idea, Alster?" Murphy asked.

"Yes, I do. And an option on some land."

"For heaven's sake!" cried Jane.

"Where is it?" asked Murphy. "Though I think we could find you a house."

"I want to be in the woods. I have optioned ten acres where the kids have been living."

"Not that awful house!" cried Jane.

"Not that awful house, no. But if we could build a new one—"

"A log cabin, I suppose."

"That, or an A-frame," said Alster seriously.

"With the kids in their shack. Be folksy, all right. Company for dinner every night."

"Oh, Jane, be fair. They've not come around except when asked. Besides, they are leaving . . ."

This surprised Murphy as well as Jane.

Where? they asked. When? What was their idea?

Alster raised his hand to silence them. "I want lemon pie for dessert," he said. "And I'll tell you all about it. I went over there last night, met them on the road, incidentally, on their way to tell us. Of course I told them about the ring. Margaret thinks I should get you a fake, Jane, and put that one in the safety deposit box."

"Alster . . ."

"It isn't a bad idea," said Murphy.

Jane was ready to scream with exasperation and curiosity. She didn't want any dessert she told the waitress who came to their table just then.

"Yes, she does," said Dr. Alster. "Lemon pie for three, and bring our coffee with it. Please?"

The girl departed, her apron bow bobbing prettily.

"Now!" said Alster, leaning back in his chair. "The kids were coming down to tell us that Mark was being transferred to the West Virginia installation."

"Does he want to go?"

"I doubt if he was asked. In the company, when offered a promotion, you take it or know that you will never have the chance again."

"So they are going to West Virginia," said Jane. "Well, they won't have much to move. They . . ."

"And Margaret is going back to school."

His companions stared at him, completely taken by surprise.

"She is," said Alster. "She thinks she can pass the entrance exams for a college near where Mark will be working. I've agreed to pay her tuition."

"You didn't!" said Jane.

"Of course I did. I hung the pill to the agreement, but I want my daughter educated."

Murphy said he thought the arrangement a fine one. Jane resented Alster's making plans behind her back.

"I didn't have a damn thing to do with it!" he cried.

"Don't tell me they thought of it themselves."

"All right, I won't tell you that. Because it was Hilda who persuaded Margaret that she should enter the college here. Now, of course—"

Jane fumed and complained. It was a big expense. Margaret should never have married. And what business was it of Hilda's . . . ?

"She made it her business," said Alster. "And I am grateful to her. She's a good friend. That's why I am seriously considering Murphy's offer. We have many friends here."

"Good and bad," said Jane grumpily. She liked to be the one to make the plans.

"Yes, good and not so good," Alster agreed. "Here's our pie!"

It was good pie. An acquaintance came by, stopped and talked to them; Alster and Murphy talked about the woman when she left. She was one of Murphy's patients. Jane, accustomed to this sort of professional discussion between the men, ate her pie and said she wanted to go home. "I don't think we have anything more to discuss," she told the men. "Alster is going to build a cabin in the woods, and work for Murphy, and it seems that I'll be going to New York alone."

"That last is up to you," said her husband, rising to draw back her chair.

"But you are going to stay here?"

"Yes. Yes, I am. That much I have decided."

Murphy clapped his hand on Alster's shoulder, said, "Good night, Jane," and walked away.

Alster asked to have his car brought around, and they drove home in silence. He had known that Jane would not like any part of his decision. She would talk about it soon enough, and often enough.

She began when they entered their house. She looked around. Her slipper toe brushed the pile of the green carpet, she looked up at the circling stairs and at the piano; she went to the glass wall and looked out at their little swimming pool, dimly lighted at night for safety's sake.

"Living where the kids have been living," she said coolly, "is definitely not your style, Alster. You haven't given much thought to me, either. When it was a matter of Mark and Margaret living in your canyon, you worried about the danger your daughter would face when left alone. What about me?"

"You'll be in New York," said Alster. "Or I suppose we'd have an apartment in Scott." He spoke cheerfully. "But I plan to do what the kids are already learning that they must do. I'll get to work."

"For Murphy."

"With Murphy. And I'll do research. Maybe more and more of that as time goes by. I can build a small lab—the possibilities are tremendous."

"For research." She was definitely not charmed with any prospects he was opening to her. "I hope your grant will help build your house."

"It will. I'll finish my six months here at the complex, and then move our things from Missouri and settle in."

"Doing research in what? The cholesterol item cannot be dragged out indefinitely."

"I'll find my field. Something like finding a substitute for saccharin. Working with Murphy may decide things for me."

"I don't think you'll like working under him."

"I don't think the position he offered means that, but if it does, I can work under him. He's a fine doctor."

"Oh, he is, he is. And you'll have some noble fights with him."

"Yes, indeed. And some good ones. I am going to bed.

If you get up early enough you can walk up the mountain with me."

He already had the telephone in hand and was calling the hospital for a check-in. Jane started for the stairs. "I feel completely abandoned," she called over her shoulder.

Alster glanced at her, but spoke into the phone.

The next morning it was raining, gently, but Alster was up very early, and he put another English muffin into the toaster when Jane came, sleepily, down the stairs.

"You're going," she said accusingly.

"Of course. I'll check things at the hospital while you finish up here, and dress. Flat-heeled shoes and light rain gear. I ll be back . . ."

He would be, too. Discontentedly, she put blackberry jam on the muffin and drank some coffee. She knew Alster, she had had this same disagreement with him before. He would make his decision and, right or wrong, stay with it.

"I'd rather move to Minnesota," she said aloud.

But she knew that they would not make such a move. Within the hour, Alster was back, talking earnestly to Joe Raithel as he came down the walk from the hospital. Jane hoped *he* was not going with them.

He was not. And Alster was promising to be back at noon. Joe could make plans of his own for the afternoon, barring some crucial development.

Jane wore a yellow poncho and looked pretty under a foul-weather hat. Alster had a rain suit, which he pulled on over his slacks and T-shirt. "The rain could stop," he predicted. "I wish we could make a day of it."

"It is a long walk."

"The site I have in mind is downhill from where the

kids are. Across the river, of course, from what you call my canyon, but it's the same canyon. There are more trees on our side."

"Your side."

He said nothing, but held out his hand to help her up a steep place. "Can you cut your own trees?" she asked.

"With the forestry's permission. I'd take down what might be needed for a clearing."

"What about plumbing?"

"Septic tank, perhaps. The river water for general use, or a well, perhaps, for us all to use. Solar heating, though we could easily have electricity."

"And Murphy would build right next door."

"No, he has his own home in Scott."

For twenty minutes they walked in silence. The perfume of the pines was all about them.

"Do you want to rest?" Alster asked her.

"I don't want to be here at all. But I was thinking, with you teamed up with Murphy, what if I should set out to get the man?"

"Murphy?" Alster asked in surprise. "The idea intrigues me," he told her. "Have you figured out how to begin, and maybe more important, what you will do if you fail?"

"I wouldn't fail," she said, clutching at a tall, weedy plant to pull her up the grade.

"All other attempts have failed. Beginning with you fifteen years ago, and the Oquist at Pemscot's birthday party."

This made her laugh. "I am not Rose Oquest," she pointed out.

"No, you are not. And you almost certainly would not use her approach."

"Musk perfume and a tight black dress, you mean."

"I know you would think of something else."

"Men usually are attracted to me."

"You bet they are. But the trouble with Murphy is, he knows you too well, Jane. Perhaps he does. And he's known you for too long."

Jane came abreast with him on a comparatively flat stretch of path. "I think I should try, just to prove you are wrong."

"And what will you do with your skunk if you catch him? *If* you do."

"Murphy has his own attractions. For women, I mean. The fact that he thinks he's impervious—"

"Why in hell do you decide that he thinks that?"

"Doesn't he?"

"He must have firsthand knowledge that he is not. But with the defense he's built up, you'll chip your pretty teeth on any such project. I don't suppose you believe me, so I can safely wish you good luck, if Murphy is what you want."

"Men never can see what women admire in other men. Just as women can't see . . ."

"I know Murphy is a virile, good-looking man. And the fact that he seems to be invulnerable to women—"

"No man is invulnerable to women."

"To women like you, you mean."

She shrugged. "All women are like me. And one will set out to get Murphy, and I predict that she will win. It might as well be me."

"I hope you're right," said Alster, stopping to take off the rain suit. The thing was hot, and the rain had tapered to a fine mist. "I'll have a great time watching you, and so will Murphy. He's just at the right age to enjoy such a hassle."

She walked on up the trail, furious with him. The least he could have done—

He caught up with her and lifted the poncho from

her head and shoulders. He folded it with his own rain gear, and put the bundle into the branches of a pine tree.

Jane watched him. They now were under too many trees for rain to get them very wet, unless the wind blew up a tornado. "Do you know something, Alster?" she asked him.

"Just a little something. What did you have in mind?"

"That you are a hateful man."

Now the woods were all about them; the tops of the tall, crested trees whispered and talked. Their path was over a deep mast of needles and pinecones. "Years and years of the stuff," murmured Alster, kicking a hole in it with his foot. Below the slope the river gleamed in the mist. A man in a red cap had pulled his small boat to the shore and was preparing to fish.

"When do we reach the site of your mountain home?" Jane asked.

"When we are through this grove of trees. There's a pleasant slope—"

"And a road, I hope."

"There's the old logging road the kids use. You've been up it."

"Not in a car."

"We'll clear a road when we build."

"We," she echoed acidly.

He laughed. "Speaking of hateful—"

"Will you do the roadwork, or pay to have it done?"

"I'm a doctor, not a day laborer, but Mark and I decided it could be done, and the house built. There is a beautiful view."

"Of money, perhaps?"

"If you are earning your own, why worry?"

"Alster . . ."

"All right, all right. We've had a good year; I shall continue to draw a good salary for six months, and I can count on a living income once I'm with Murphy. The grant is for research facilities, time, and study—and it will help with our expenses."

"Including college tuition for Margaret. What about her clothes and other—?"

"Mark has a job; she says she can earn something herself, and of course she can. The tuition is all of it."

"It's never happened before."

"No, it has not. But I am feeling better about that marriage. She's stuck it out for several weeks—they are going to leave us their solar stove, by the way."

"Clap hands, clap hands!"

"Jane . . ."

"Do I have to live here?" she asked, seeing the clearing ahead of them. The view indeed was beautiful, the river, the small canyon, and the mountains rising in a semicircle of rocks and trees, light and shadow against the morning sky.

"You don't have to live here," Alster told her calmly, "but you will."

She agreed. "Yes, I suppose I shall. Do you plan a nice house?"

"For your convenience? Yes, it will be nice."

She stopped and looked behind them at the way they had come, below them at the boxlike home of Mark and Margaret.

"I understand they have deep snow some winters."

"They do. And we probably should have an apartment in town against such emergencies."

"That's a good idea," she agreed. Then she shot him a glance. "A one-room efficiency?" she suggested.

"It's all we'd need."

"Mmmm. And knowing my luck, I'll find myself

abandoned out here on the mountain with the bears and the chipmunks. Oh, yes, and the solar stove."

"You can follow your plan of going to New York."

"And you wouldn't miss me."

"Of course I would miss you."

"Maybe," she amended. "Or, maybe, I could be your office nurse, and Murphy's."

"Working for the man would be the last way to get the man, sweetheart. Besides, he has a nurse. Two of them, in fact."

"Does he keep busy? Will you keep busy?"

"I think so, in both cases. The company is closing the hospital, but they will continue to pay for medical care under approved services. At least one of the Scott hospitals is planning to expand. Yes, there will be plenty of work. I think Murphy and I have both satisfied the complex employees as doctors. This will be our home, but I, at least, will be in town for better than half of the time. We'll continue our country club membership and the Friday-night dinners."

"Are you coaxing me?"

"Not at all."

She laughed, somewhat wryly. "Knowing how stubborn and hateful you can be, why do you suppose I'll stay with you?"

"For the same reason you pursued me eighteen years ago." He sat down, and patted the length of the fallen tree for her to rest, too.

"I caught you," she reminded him.

"Because I was off on a pursuit of my own."

"I remember. Something to do with Down's syndrome."

"That's right. And long before I was finished, I found myself about to father a daughter, and married to you."

She touched his arm. "It hasn't been too bad, has it?"

"Yes, it has, at times. But we stuck it out. Our friends thought we wouldn't."

"What did they know? You did good work, I learned a lot of things, and Margaret isn't too bad a daughter. Stubborn like you, of course."

"Of course. And of course it has not been bad, except when I get hateful."

"As you do, just to devil me."

He drew a deep breath. "Don't the trees smell wonderful?"

"They do. There's a dead one over there."

"Mmmm. Probably it was a seedling before the Civil War; it's lived its life and has been allowed to die. One day it will fall, and we shall miss it as we do any old friend. And that's the way it should be."

Jane sighed. "Whoever called you a bore," she said softly, "the other night at dinner, was dead right. You can be one."

"I know it," he said cheerfully.

"And sadistic."

"Oh, sure. That's the most fun." He stood up, and reached his hand to help her. "Let's go home. I'm hungry for another breakfast."

She laughed. "We do understand each other," she agreed. "I insult you, and you always agree."

They started back the way they had come. The path through the woods was darkening with the rain clouds that were gathering again. They claimed their rain gear and put it on. "You know," said Jane, when they once more began to walk, "thinking about seducing Murphy Anderson—"

Alster snorted.

"He must not be invulnerable, or wasn't at one time in his life. He must have fallen in love with some woman, and surrendered to her."

"What makes you think so?" Alster asked, his tone interested.

"Well," said Jane, kneeling to tie her canvas shoe. "There's Alan. No stork brought him."

"No. One didn't," said Alster, his tone so strange that she glanced up at him.

"What happened to the boy's mother?" she asked.

"I don't know."

"Well, of course you know. You and Murphy— Did she die, or divorce the man, or what?"

"I really do not know, Jane."

"But something must have gone bad with his marriage. I have blamed the mother for deserting the child."

"I think she deserves some blame."

"Murphy stayed with the boy. Most parents would have institutionalized him."

"Many do, yes."

"He must be impossible to live with— Does Murphy have someone?"

"He has a couple taking care of his home, and of Alan."

"But the boy gets away. I understand he did all sorts of damage to one of the complex buildings."

"Yes, and Murphy resigned his job, moved to Scott, and we came here."

"If the boy is incorrigible . . ."

"The boy has many problems."

"And Murphy blames himself."

"No. No, he doesn't."

"Why not?"

"Alan is not Murphy's son, Jane. Shall we make a run for it, or wait here under the trees? That rain looks mighty wet."

She watched the shower for a moment. "We'll wait," she said, "and while we wait you can tell me about Alan, and Murphy, and the whole thing. The man has given his life to that awful boy."

Alster moved back a little for further shelter. The shower would not last long.

"Murphy is a doctor," he said quietly. "Alan was born to a woman—she and her husband were friends of his, and of ours. This was about the time we went to Arizona."

"I knew them?"

"Of course you knew them. And you will guess their names. They were somewhat older than we were, but lived in the same apartment building. The child was born—the term is "defective." I had done my Down's and other chromosome detection work—something like the work I am planning on heredity and the part it plays in Alpha and Beta cholesterol—"

She touched his arm.

He nodded. "Yes. Murphy asked me to come and examine the child, tell his parents what hope they had of his being—of having a viable future. The father had just been named concert master of a big symphony orchestra."

Jane was watching him, and now her soft lips formed a name.

Alster nodded. "The public mind," he said, "then, even more than now, makes a connection between Down's and criminally aggressive behavior."

"She was too old to have a child."

"She was forty-five, yes. And the child—"

"Alan."

"Alan. The parents promised to abandon the baby. I could give them little hope of a peaceful, prideful future. Murphy told them that they could not desert the pitiful creature he was. 'Then you take him,' said the mother."

"And he did."

"He did. But not right away. Like most defective infants, Alan had multiple problems. Intussusception, nervous difficulties. He was not quite autistic—there was no withdrawal."

"And Murphy adopted him."

"Not right away. The father was ready to work with the child, but the mother was completely revolted."

"Oh, dear. And of course the father's music—"

"Yes. He was a fine musician, and he had the most perfect bow arm I ever saw."

Jane clutched his sleeve. "But wasn't he killed, Alster?"

"Yes. Yes, he was. An automobile accident. So then Murphy took over. I, too, thought that we should . . ."

"We?" She turned to stare at him in horror.

"We," he said firmly. "You and I. We had an organized home, a mother and father for that unfortunate child."

"Alster, you're crazy!"

"Well, that's never been proven. But Murphy was against my taking Alan, largely because of Margaret."

"Well, I should think so!"

"But we have cared for him, given him medical care and an education. He's done well under play therapy. Murphy's had the hardest half of the deal. He has had him in the home and is legally responsible—"

"But you help."

Alster stood up. "I think the worst of the rain is over. Let's get going."

But she did not move. "I want the rest of it," she said. "Did the mother consent to Murphy's adopting the boy?"

"Yes."

"She could have made things pretty sticky."

"She didn't."

"And—how long has this gone on? While you were in the Indian Service. And Mike—"

"Yes, he helped out; he was old enough to take over a time or two and give Murph a chance to do some brush-up work."

"And that's why he went into the priesthood."

"Yes. He'll work with such children. Perhaps Alan can help him."

Jane rose slowly to her feet. "You damn men," she said softly, clearly. "You damn, damn men. And you've let me call you hateful—"

"I have been hateful, sometimes. But don't give me the credit. Murphy's had the heaviest burden, by far. And he couldn't marry—"

"Did he want to?"

"He's an attractive man. Normal. But he could not bring a woman into that home. And he would not separate from Alan."

"Some day—Oh, God, I thought he was using Alan as a foil against the Oquest woman."

"And you."

She nodded, and started down the trail, holding his arm. The rain had made the rocks slippery. "I tried," she admitted.

"I know. And you would have made him a good wife."

"I've not always been a good one to you."

"He'd make you be a good one to him. He's a stronger man than I am. He stays with a thing. I get angry and quit."

"Is he teaching you? This working with him in Scott—"

"He's forcing me now. He says it is time I learned the things I need to learn."

As they walked, she thought that over. "I don't know if I admire him more, or you."

"Under the circumstances, it had better be me."

In his pocket, the beeper began to chatter. He cursed a bit, then, "Can you run the rest of the way?"

"Kiss me, first."

Surprised, he did kiss her. "Now let's run," she said. "The hospital comes first."

"You bet."

"Then go ahead. I'll make it home."

And in the mist she stood there, watching the doctor, the man, the damned man.